The Daring
of Della Dupree
By Natasha Lowe

Also by Natasha Lowe

The Power of Poppy Pendle
The Courage of Cat Campbell
The Marvelous Magic of Miss Mabel

Lucy Castor Finds Her Sparkle

The Daring
of Della Dupree

By Natasha Lowe

A PAULA WISEMAN BOOK
Simon & Schuster Books for Young Readers
NEW YORK   LONDON   TORONTO   SYDNEY   NEW DELHI

SIMON & SCHUSTER BOOKS FOR YOUNG READERS
An imprint of Simon & Schuster Children's Publishing Division
1230 Avenue of the Americas, New York, New York 10020
This book is a work of fiction. Any references to historical events,
real people, or real places are used fictitiously. Other names, characters, places,
and events are products of the author's imagination, and any resemblance to actual
events or places or persons, living or dead, is entirely coincidental.
For information about special discounts for bulk purchases, please contact Simon &
Schuster Special Sales at 1-866-506-1949 or business@simonandschuster.com.
The Simon & Schuster Speakers Bureau can bring authors to your live event.
For more information or to book an event, contact the Simon & Schuster Speakers
Bureau at 1-866-248-3049 or visit our website at www.simonspeakers.com.
Jacket design by Chloë Foglia
Interior design by Tom Daly
The text for this book was set in Cochin LT Std.
Manufactured in the United States of America
0620 BVG
First Edition
2 4 6 8 10 9 7 5 3 1
Library of Congress Cataloging-in-Publication Data
Names: Lowe, Natasha, author.
Title: The daring of Della Dupree / Natasha Lowe.
Description: First edition. | New York : Simon & Schuster Books for Young Readers,
[2020] | "A Paula Wiseman Book." | Audience: Ages 8–12. | Audience: Grades 4–6. |
Summary: Della Dupree feels she is nothing like her namesake, the founder of prestigious
Ruthersfield Academy, but one day she finds herself alone in the year 1223 with nothing
but her witchcraft to save her. Includes recipes and craft instructions.
Identifiers: LCCN 2019028332 (print) | LCCN 2019028333 (eBook) |
ISBN 9781534443679 (hardback) | ISBN 9781534443693 (eBook)
Subjects: CYAC: Witches—Fiction. | Magic—Fiction. | Time travel—Fiction.
| Self-realization—Fiction. | Schools—Fiction.
Classification: LCC PZ7.L9627 Dar 2020 (print) | LCC PZ7.L9627 (eBook) |
DDC [Fic]—dc23
LC record available at https://lccn.loc.gov/2019028332
LC eBook record available at https://lccn.loc.gov/2019028333

For Mary Kay, Candace, Heather, and Steve

On Saturdays, after buying her walnut bread, Clara Bell would sit by the canal with Cat, discussing early magic in Pagan times and the evolution of witchcraft through the ages. When Cat had trouble remembering important facts, Clara Bell taught her some useful tricks. "Fourteen four, fourteen four, wands were drawn on the Penine Moor," or, "Twelve twenty-three, twelve twenty-three, Ruthersfield was founded by Witch Dupree."

—from *The Courage of Cat Campbell*

Chapter One

······································

Della

"DELLA DUPREE, PAY ATTENTION," MISS BARLOW SNAPPED. "This is a history of magic class, and you've been staring inside your pocket for the last forty-five minutes." She tapped her wand against her thigh. "So I'd like to know what you have in there."

Della didn't answer, although she wanted to point out that it hadn't been for the whole forty-five minutes, only the last ten. However, she was too scared of Miss Barlow to say this. She thought about practicing the vanishing spell they had learned in potions class yesterday, but disappearing would only get her into more trouble.

"Well, Miss Dupree? I'm waiting."

"A duck," Della whispered, feeling her cheeks start to burn. "A tiny, baby duckling that doesn't have a mother. He imprinted on me, Miss Barlow, and I have to keep him warm. I've put him under a sleep enchantment so he can rest," she explained. "His name's Pickle. He's a common scoter duck, and it's extra important to keep him safe because common scoter ducks aren't actually common at all. They're on the endangered list." Della could hear Melanie Sloane and Cassie Watkins laughing behind her, and she shook her hair forward to hide her face.

"Pickle is it?" Miss Barlow narrowed her eyes. "And last week it was a turtledove with a broken wing called Flutter."

"Also on the endangered list," Della murmured.

"And before that, if I remember correctly, a bunny with a torn ear that you stuck back together with healing tape from the nurse's office? Very expensive healing tape I might add, which we like to save for broomstick accidents."

Della nodded, wishing everyone would stop staring at her.

Miss Barlow stalked over and stood beside Della's desk. "You're not even on the right page, Della," she sighed, glancing down at *Magic in the Middle Ages*. "Per-

haps if you paid more attention in class, your grades would improve."

"I'm very sorry, Miss Barlow."

"Do you even know what we're studying?"

"How Ruthersfield Academy was started?"

"Yes, indeed, and I would have thought that you, of all people, would be interested in the founding of our great school," the history teacher said. "Which as we all know was the first accredited school for magic in this country. Set up in?" She looked around the class, and the girls chanted back at her, "Twelve twenty-three."

"By?" Miss Barlow held out her arms, and Della's classmates chorused, with a sprinkling of laughter, "Della Dupree!"

Della winced, wishing for the twelve thousandth time that her parents had named her Isabel or Lucy or anything other than Della. But her mother had loved the name, so that's what she had been called. In fact, as far as Della knew, she wasn't even related to the original Della Dupree who started Ruthersfield Academy. There were Duprees all over Yorkshire and Lancashire, but the only witch Della was aware of in her family happened to be a potion maker called Agatha, four generations back, who had run a small magic shop on Oxford Street in London. "I mean we never actually thought you'd turn out to be a witch!" her mother often said. Although when Della amazingly showed signs of magic at five years old, turning her bathwater into lime jelly and floating out of the tub on an enormous green bubble, her parents were understandably thrilled. It had to be fate, they decided. As if calling their daughter Della had been a good-luck charm, since she'd inherited the magic gene at a time when fewer and fewer witches were being born each year. Except, in Della's eyes, all she had inherited was the lifelong burden of being named after one of the world's most famous witches. And it wasn't an easy name to live up to.

She was nothing like that Della Dupree, who must have been brilliant and outspoken with a loud commanding voice. Probably fearless, too, Della reckoned, picturing her as tall and statuesque with a cloud of dark red curls. About as different from her own skinny frame and thin, pale hair as you could get.

"No more animals in school, Miss Dupree. I don't care how endangered they are. Is that clear?" Miss Barlow said. Della nodded, wanting to point out that there weren't any rules in the handbook about carrying animals around in your pockets, but she hated speaking up in class, with everyone staring and listening.

"I'm sure that's why my eyes have been watering all day," Melanie whispered to Cassie, but loud enough for Della to hear. "I cannot be around feathers." Cassie gave an explosive laugh, which she turned into a fake-sounding cough.

"All right, calm down, girls." Miss Barlow clapped her hands. "Your homework assignment is to come up with a short presentation for the class, written from the point of view of the great Della Dupree. This could be a letter, a descriptive passage, a monologue . . ."

"About why we like to rescue little animals?" Melanie Sloane asked innocently, making Della sink down farther in her chair.

"About what it was like for Della, growing up in the Middle Ages," Miss Barlow said, giving Melanie a sharp frown. "Be creative. There isn't a lot written on our founder, but I want you all to think about what it meant to be a witch back then. We know witches were feared and locked up, so how did that affect Della when she was your age? Were her parents supportive? Was she allowed to practice magic at all before Ruthersfield existed? What did her friends think? Put yourselves back in the thirteenth century and give me your best work, to be shared with the class tomorrow." Loud groans could be heard, and Miss Barlow raised her voice. "Now pack up quietly, please, because I have a meeting to attend." She swooped out of the room, obviously remembering she had left her briefcase behind, because a moment later it floated into the air and sped after her.

The girls shoved back their chairs and started to pack up their backpacks. Della saw Melanie and Cassie staring at Katrin Einarsdottir as she stuffed her history of magic book into an oversize floppy knitted bag made from gold and purple wool. It had long, knitted handles that she draped over her shoulder, and in a syrupy voice Melanie said, "That's a lovely bag, Katrin."

"Thanks," Katrin said, not sure whether Melanie was being sarcastic or not. She had arrived from Iceland last year, and although she spoke excellent English, she sometimes found it hard to tell when people (particularly Melanie) were making fun of her. "My grandpa made it for me." She looked a little sad, like she might be missing her grandpa, and Della wanted to ask if a lot of people's grandpas knitted in Iceland, and how often Katrin got to see him. But her mouth went dry at the thought of talking to Katrin in front of Melanie, so she didn't say anything.

"Did he knit you that wand case, too?" Melanie said, eyeing the woolly purple-and-gold cover for Katrin's wand and trying to keep a straight face. "In case it gets cold? You probably have woolly broomstick covers in Iceland too, don't you?"

"Broomstick covers?" Katrin looked puzzled. "I don't think so."

Cassie snickered, and Katrin turned away, realizing the girls were being mean.

"Do you think he'd make me one?" Melanie asked. "In the school colors, just like yours?"

"Or knit me a bow for my hat?" Cassie suggested. They were always making fun of poor Katrin—her clothes, her accent—or pointing out that no Icelandic witch had ever won a Noblet prize, the awards given out once a year for the most impressive advancements in witchcraft.

"She shouldn't even be in Ruthersfield," Melanie was always murmuring about Katrin. "It's not like they don't have witch schools over there. My cousin is an amazing witch, and she didn't get into Ruthersfield because there was no room. But Katrin gets in. That's so not fair."

Della wished she had the courage to say something, to tell them to be quiet and leave Katrin alone. So what if she came from Iceland? Why did that give Melanie the right to be so horrible to her, making all those jokes about people from Iceland being stupid and wearing woolly ear warmers? But Della knew if she tried to speak up, Melanie would make fun of her, too. It seemed ridiculous that Melanie should have the power to decide who was going to be popular and who couldn't have any friends. But the truth was she did, because Della and the rest of the girls were scared of her.

Della tried to send Katrin a look of sympathy as she slung her backpack over her shoulder. She always smiled at Katrin whenever she could and never minded being paired up with her in potions class. But Katrin had her head down, and not knowing what else to do, Della joined Anna and Sophie on their way out of the classroom, checking that Pickle was still safely tucked up in her pocket.

"I don't know how I'm going to finish my history homework," Anna grumbled. "I've got broomstick gymnastics after school, and it's going to be a really long practice, because we have a big competition this weekend."

"At least you've done your reading," Della said as they walked across the great hall toward the cafeteria. "I've been so busy taking care of Pickle, I know absolutely nothing about the Middle Ages. Or Witch Dupree for that matter." She couldn't help feeling that Miss Barlow would expect her presentation to be extra good, just because she shared the same name as their founder.

"It can't have been easy starting up a magic school when everyone hated witches so much," Anna said.

"Oh, I'm sure it wasn't that bad," Sophie replied. "We all know witches are amazing!"

Della wished Miss Barlow had given the class another assignment. All this attention on Witch Dupree made her uncomfortable, as if people were looking at her more closely now too, silently comparing them. "But I do wonder what she was like," Della murmured, curious to know if she had anything in common with the famous witch at all.

"Are you talking about Della Dupree?" Melanie asked, walking over with Cassie. "I bet she was off fighting dragons. Showing everyone how brave witches were. Not being all sensitive, carrying baby ducks around in her pocket!" Cassie giggled, and Melanie added, "I'm only joking, Della."

Della smiled, pretending not to mind, which was what all the girls did when Melanie made fun of them: act like they weren't bothered.

"How is Pickle doing?" Anna asked at lunch, taking a bite of shepherd's pie.

"I'm not sure. He's so tiny. I'll feel better when he wakes up and starts eating." Della prodded at a carrot on her plate, not feeling particularly hungry. "I really wish we had an animal-magic program here like they do at that witch school in Germany," she said. "I watched a whole show on it last week, and it was so amazing. They feed abandoned kittens with unicorn milk, because it's way more nutritious than regular milk, and they have these cobweb hammocks to rock baby birds in. There's a phoenix that blows constant hot air in the room to keep the animals warm, and special enchantments to mimic their mothers' noises. It's genius."

"Why don't you talk to Ms. Cray about setting one up?" Anna suggested.

"Oh, she'd hate the idea. *'Mucking about with animals is not an academic subject,'*" Della mimicked in her best headmistress's voice. "Plus, you know she terrifies me. I avoid speaking to her at all costs."

"Well, the girls would love it," Sophie said.

"Not Melanie," Della pointed out. "She's allergic to just about every single animal there is."

"Melanie's not the boss of everyone," Anna muttered as Katrin wandered down the aisle, looking for a place to sit.

"You should probably sit by the window," Melanie called out sweetly. "It's nice and cold over there. Like Iceland!"

Della glanced around, waiting for someone to say something. But no one did, and Miss Harding, the teacher on lunch duty, clearly hadn't heard.

"She's so mean," Della whispered as poor Katrin found an empty table. Anna and Sophie nodded in agreement. "We should go and sit with her," Della said, knowing they wouldn't do this, but it made her feel better to say it.

"Then Melanie will turn everyone against us," Anna murmured.

"Honestly, if it wasn't against the rules, I swear I'd turn Melanie into the weasel rat she is," Della hissed.

Anna paled and made the sign of the sickle moon above her head. "Don't say that, Della, not even as a joke. You'd get sent straight to Scrubs Prison if you did such a thing." And with that sobering thought the girls finished their lunch in silence.

Chapter Two

The House on Button Street

WHEN THE LAST BELL RANG AFTER SPELL-CHANTING class, Della clattered down the wide stone steps of the academy, desperate to get home and try to feed Pickle some unicorn milk using the tiny dropper she had borrowed from the potions lab. She grabbed her broom from the broom shed and took off with a shaky wobble.

"Hat on properly, Della Dupree," Ms. Randal barked. "And tuck your shirt in. You represent Ruthersfield Academy. It is not acceptable to look like a scarecrow." Della had Ms. Randal for fortune-telling this term, and she usually never shouted. But for the past two weeks, since her extremely ancient poodle had died, she seemed to be in a perpetual bad mood. Being an animal lover herself, Della could understand this, and she tried to not mind Ms. Randal's grumpiness.

"Sorry," Della called down, straightening her witch's hat while keeping one hand firmly on the broomstick. Della's class had been flying for only a couple of months now, since aviation lessons didn't start until year four, and the girls were still rather unsteady.

"Don't forget history homework," Sophie shouted, swooping off in the other direction. Della could hear her friend singing to herself, "Twelve twenty-three, twelve twenty-three, Ruthersfield was founded by Witch Dupree!"

"As if I could forget," Della muttered. She was used to the comments she often got when filling out forms or telling people her name.

"Wow, Della Dupree! Like the Della Dupree who founded Ruthersfield! And you're a witch too! That's so great."

Except it wasn't great at all. Not that her parents ever said they expected amazing things from her, but Della was sure that they did, and the weight of her name felt as heavy as the history book in her backpack, tipping her slight frame off balance as she flew. Plus, just the thought of all that reading about the Middle Ages made Della's brain ache. To cheer herself up, she decided to stop in at Poppy's bakery for a treat. It was hard to resist the delicious smells that wafted out of the little bakery every day, and Della often spent her pocket money on a honeycomb cupcake or some caramel crunch cookies.

Angling her broomstick a smidgeon to the left, she headed toward the canal, breathing in the rich scent of chocolate on the breeze. The afternoon was deliciously mild for early April, and Della enjoyed looking down, seeing Potts Bottom spread out below her. Shops and houses crammed along the narrow, cobbled streets and the canal running right through the center of town. She wobbled as two sixth formers whizzed by. "Too slow," one of them yelled back at her. "You're going to cause a pileup."

"Better than losing control and breaking my neck," Della gasped, although the girls were too far ahead to hear. She flew down the canal path, following the smell of chocolate butter bread, which Poppy only made on Wednesdays, and landed outside the small stone bakery that most people felt was the heart and soul of the village.

Photos of Poppy's daughter, Cat, hung on the walls. She was a member of the perilous High Flyers, a broomstick rescue team that flew all over the world, saving people from dangerous situations. Della had only met Cat a few times and attempted to talk to her once. It was not a meeting she liked to remember, as she was so tongue-tied and intimidated she couldn't speak a word. Both Cat and Poppy had inherited the rare magic gene, but Poppy had given up witchcraft many years ago to open a bakery, which everyone in Potts Bottom agreed was an extremely sensible decision.

Standing on tiptoe, Della said, "Two honeycomb cupcakes, an almond macaroon, and three chocolate melt-aways, please. And a caramel cookie," she added, brushing a wisp of hair out of her face.

Poppy smiled down at her from behind the counter, a dusting of flour on her nose. Her long braid had more gray in it than brown these days, but her eyes were still warm and sparkly. "I don't know where you put it all, Della."

"This is stress eating," Della said. "Because I have a homework assignment I really don't want to do. We're studying magic in the Middle Ages, and I'm supposed to give a presentation tomorrow in front of the whole class, which makes me feel sick to my stomach."

"What sort of presentation?" Poppy asked.

"It could be a letter, or a speech." Della sighed. "It doesn't really matter as long as it's from the point of view of Della Dupree. You know, *the* Della Dupree."

"Ahhh! Poor you." Poppy slipped an extra choco-late melt-away into the bag. "She's always been one of Cat's heroes."

"I bet," Della said, thinking that Cat and Witch Dupree would probably have had a lot in common. In fact it should have been Cat who was named after the founder of Ruthersfield and not her, Della decided, aware that she could never measure up.

As Della turned to go, the doorbell jingled and Katrin walked in. Before Della had a chance to smile, Katrin quickly looked away, as if expecting Della not to speak to her.

"Hi, Katrin," Della said softly, uncomfortable that Katrin didn't see her as a friend. Della swallowed, wanting to say something about Melanie, about how horrible she could be and that they were all scared of her. But she couldn't think of the right words, and then it was too late and Katrin had walked up to the counter. So Della left without saying anything.

Eating on broomsticks was strictly forbidden since a year five girl had knocked out a pedestrian with an apple last year, so Della gobbled down her cup-cake before flying home, saving the cookies for later. Remembering not to fly above the tree line, Della wobbled along Button Street, waving to Mrs. Cox, who was hanging out her washing.

"Looking good, Della!" Mrs. Cox called, grinning up at her.

"Thanks, Mrs. Cox. I'm finally getting the hang of it."

The row of little brick houses were snuggled together, and Della could see her older brothers, Sam and Henry, kicking a soccer ball around their tiny front yard. They dived dramatically to one side, covering their heads as Della landed rather bumpily on the lawn.

"I'm not that bad," Della said, checking to make sure Pickle was okay.

Sam grinned. "We're just kidding, Sprite!" "Sprite" was Della's nickname, given more for her tiny build than her magical powers. Not that she was particularly short for an eleven-year-old, but compared to thirteen-year-old Sam and fifteen-year-old Henry, who were both almost six feet tall, Della couldn't help feeling slightly undersized. Like she wasn't quite big enough to fill up her place in the family.

"When are you going to take us for a broomstick ride?" Henry asked, picking Della up and carrying her into the house. As he opened the front door, they were met with the lovely smell of lasagna baking.

"Can't. You know it's against the rules. If Ms. Cray found out, I'd be expelled."

"You have so many rules at that school, it's ridiculous,"

Henry said, putting Della down on a chair in the kitchen.

Their mother stood at the stove, and hanging above her was a cobweb net filled with three abandoned baby bats that Della had found and brought home.

"Nice day?" Della's mum said, smiling at Della as she jumped onto the floor. Immediately, Robbie, the youngest Dupree, came barreling over, holding a piece of bread and honey, and wrapped his hands around Della's legs.

"Not the best," Della admitted. "But better now I know we've got lasagna."

"It's all those rules," Sam joked. "Of course school is no fun."

"Well, being a witch is a big deal," Della continued, brushing back Robbie's long tangle of curls, which at three years old he stubbornly refused to have cut. "They don't let you ever forget that. How we have to live up to our magic. It's exhausting."

Waving his arms about, Henry bowed and said, "Let us honor the incredible, the amazing, the extraordinary Della Dupree."

"Oh, if only," Della sighed, feeling far more ordinary than extraordinary.

"Well, we think you're wonderful," Mrs. Dupree said. "Wouldn't change a thing."

Except my name, Della couldn't help thinking.

"Did Pickle like school?" Robbie asked in a muffled voice. He planted a kiss on Della's kneecap. "I missed you, Della."

"I missed you too, Lion," Della said fondly, using the name they sometimes called him because of his shaggy mane of hair. "And I think Pickle is glad to be home, actually." She lifted the duckling out of her pocket, and with Robbie's help (which meant constantly stroking and kissing Pickle) she nestled the baby bird into a teapot filled with hay.

Mrs. Dupree glanced at the wall clock. "Goodness, boys, you're late for soccer practice. And, Della," she added pleadingly, "is there any way you can move this lot up to your bedroom?" She gestured at the bat net Della had strung up and the basket with Flutter in it floating about the room. Della had thought it would be nice for her turtledove to feel like he was flying while his wing healed, even if he couldn't fly. "It's supposed to be a kitchen," Mrs. Dupree pointed out, "not an animal sanctuary."

"Well, I can't keep them at school, and they'd be lonely in my bedroom," Della said, waving her wand at the net and murmuring, "Lulaballo." The cobweb hammock started to swing gently. "They love being down here with you and Robbie, Mum."

"Oh do they," Mrs. Dupree muttered, but Della

could tell she was smiling. "Do you have homework, Della? I was hoping you could watch Lion for me so I don't have to drag him along to soccer practice, since your dad's working late."

"A bit," Della admitted, not wanting to tell her mother what it was about. Any mention of Witch Dupree always made her feel ridiculously inadequate. "I'll do it after I've fed Pickle." With Robbie breathing over her, she dripped a little unicorn milk into the baby duck's mouth, tucked him back up in his teapot, then took *Magic in the Middle Ages* and a rather sticky Lion upstairs to her room.

Lying on her bed with Robbie nestled beside her, Della opened the book.

"I'm not talking, Della, so you can read."

"Thank you, Lion."

"I'm a quiet lion," Robbie whispered. "Can you tell me a story?"

"When I've finished this, okay?"

"Hurry up," Robbie said, pulling off his socks.

Della had to admit it would be nice to discover even one tiny thing that she shared with Witch Dupree. Maybe their founder loved animals? Or maybe, just maybe she wasn't as courageous as everyone seemed to believe? She must have been scared of some stuff, Della reasoned, starting to read. There were several descriptions of life in the Middle Ages, a great deal about witches being feared and misunderstood, and a small mention of how Della Dupree, with her courage and determination, managed to start the first school for magic in the country. "Not much has been written about Witch Dupree after the founding of Ruthersfield," Della read, "which, of course, has led many scholars to speculate what might have happened to her. We will never know the answer to this."

Robbie started doing somersaults up and down the bed while Della flipped through a few more pages, scanning them for anything of interest. This was so frustrating. It was like reading about a superhero, not a real person. She stopped at the end of the chapter, the last paragraph catching her eye. "One source that best describes magic at this time is *The Book of Spells*, an original work from the thirteenth century, which is kept in the Ruthersfield Library. In it are rare conversations with Witch Dupree and some unusual descriptions of magic."

That's what I have to look at, Della thought, giving a little shiver of excitement. If she wanted to find out what Witch Dupree was really like, it would be in this book. People usually talked about themselves in conversations, how they truly felt about things, not just how courageous they were. Of course it would be in the restricted section, where all the really old books were kept, but it was worth a try. And being friends with the librarian couldn't hurt.

Since Robbie was clearly getting restless, Della put down *Magic in the Middle Ages* and they read stories and played with her stuffed animals until she heard the boys clatter through the door from soccer practice, kicking their boots off in the hallway. They were arguing about something, and Robbie clamped his hands over his ears. He didn't like arguments. Above the noise came her mother's calm voice, "No fighting, boys. Use your words to sort it out." In the same breath she called upstairs, "Supper, Della and Robbie. And please can you get Pickle off the table?"

"Coming," Della yelled back down. Miss Barlow would be so impressed when she found out that Della had been doing some research on her own. Perhaps she'd come across one of Witch Dupree's favorite spells and share it with the class. Or maybe, Della found herself hoping, she'd discover that their founder was actually terrified of dragons, or of flying in the dark, or of standing up to people, and didn't always feel quite so confident on the inside.

Chapter Three

···

The Book of Spells

DELLA HAD PLANNED TO GET TO SCHOOL EARLY THE next day so she could go to the library before class. But by the time she had fed the bats, taken Flutter outside for a test flight (he made it halfway across the yard before heading right back to his box), and tried to get Pickle to drink more unicorn milk (which all took five times as long with Robbie helping), she was ten minutes late for her spells and charms lesson.

The second Della walked through the classroom door, music began playing and firework holograms shot into the air. The word "welcome" wrote itself across the room in purple and gold sparkles.

"How nice of you to join us," Miss Dent said, ignoring Della's surprise and gesturing for her to sit down.

"We're learning about time-release spells," Sophie whispered as Della slipped into her seat.

"Indeed we are," Miss Dent said rather crisply. "And there will be a test on Monday, so pay attention, Miss Dupree."

"I'm sorry I'm late," Della apologized, trying to figure out what had just happened.

"As I was saying, girls," Miss Dent continued. "You can time a spell to start working at the exact moment of your choosing." She pointed her wand at the door. "Like you just witnessed. I set my welcome spell to go off when the next person walked into the room. Which happened to be you, Miss Dupree."

"Ahh." Della nodded, suddenly understanding. She was still feeling rather fuzzy-headed and wished she'd had time to stop in at Poppy's for a lemon poppy seed muffin.

"It's very easy to do," Miss Dent explained. "You just weave the time and date into your spell when you cast it." The girls spent the rest of class setting up time-activated enchantments, so every few minutes someone turned invisible or a pencil case floated around the room, much to the amusement of year four.

"Practice for homework, please," Miss Dent instructed over the bell.

As the girls trooped off to math, Della heard Melanie whisper to Cassie, "You know what I'm going to do? Send Katrin back to Iceland next Tuesday at midnight! She'd arrive in her woolly pajamas!" Some of the other girls laughed, and feeling uncomfortable, Della hurried away from Melanie, not wanting to be anywhere near her. She hoped Katrin hadn't heard, but it was hard to tell, because Katrin was walking with her head down as usual.

Math was Della's least-favorite subject, and, after being handed back a C-plus on a quiz and listening to Miss Heathcliff drone on about how to divide and multiply different amounts of potions, she was thrilled to be chosen as a messenger, missing the last few minutes of class.

"Please ask Mrs. Gibbons if she would kindly come up and fix this window as soon as possible," Miss Heathcliff instructed, waving a hand in front of her face. "It's like a furnace in here, and I cannot go another moment without air."

Della nodded and leaped up, racing off before Miss Heathcliff could change her mind. After delivering the message to Mrs. Gibbons, the school caretaker, she went straight to the fortune-telling room to wait for the others to arrive. Thankfully, they were moving on from foot reading today (similar to palm reading but could tell you about your past). This was a huge relief to all the girls, because running your fingers over your partner's sweaty feet was not exactly pleasant.

Walking into the room, Della noticed right away that the cabinet behind Ms. Randal's desk stood open. This was where the time-travel amulets were kept, fossilized dragon's eyes that hung from chains of moon gold and could take you wherever you wanted. None of the girls were allowed to go near the amulets without strict supervision from Ms. Randal, who once a year organized a prearranged field trip, often to Leonardo da Vinci's study, because he had a strong fascination with time travel. But these excursions always took place at the end of the school year, so why was the cabinet open now?

A sudden movement caught her eye, and Della gave a startled gasp as the fortune-telling teacher appeared in front of her. She looked rather windswept with unusually pink cheeks and gray hair escaping from the two fat braids she always wore, giving her the appearance of a slightly haggard twelve-year-old. Ms. Randal's eyes were glassy and unfocused, and when Della called her name, she didn't seem to hear right away. Della stared at the fossilized dragon's eye hanging around Ms. Randal's neck, and she realized with a shock that their fortune-telling teacher had been time traveling.

"Della," Ms. Randal murmured, her pink cheeks turning even pinker. She smoothed down her braids. "You're—you're early."

"I had to take a message for Miss Heathcliff," Della said, feeling uncomfortable.

"Oh dear, I—I suppose you're wondering what I'm doing?" Ms. Randal slipped off the necklace. Her voice wobbled a little, and her eyes were wet with tears. "Well, it's my last time visiting. I told Tammy that, and he understands."

"Your poodle Tammy?"

"I've been traveling back to his puppy days," Ms. Randal confessed. "Mostly at night. Taking him for walks along the canal."

"You have?"

"I have, and I know it has to stop." Ms. Randal blew her nose. "So that's where I was just now, telling Tammy good-bye."

"Oh, Ms. Randal," Della said, thinking that this was the most heartbreaking thing she'd ever heard.

"No, no, I'm fine," Ms. Randal said stoically. She put the necklace back in the cupboard and shut the door with a firm click. "And I'd appreciate it if you didn't say anything about this, Della."

"Of course not," Della said as the rest of the class burst in.

"Take your seats," Ms. Randal called out, waiting for the girls to settle. When they were all at their desks, she pulled back her shoulders and announced, "Today we look forward. No more messing about in the past." Della had a strong sense she was talking about herself here and not their foot gazing. "In single file, please come up, and I will hand you a crystal ball."

"But no one uses them anymore," Melanie said. "They're so old-fashioned."

"A Ruthersfield girl needs to know the basics," Ms. Randal replied tartly, and for the next forty-five minutes Della learned how to hold, gaze into, and read a crystal ball.

"That was so boring and pointless," Melanie complained after class as the girls poured into the corridor. "Most witches use mirror gazing or water predicting these days."

"I bet they still use crystal balls in Iceland," Cassie said.

"I bet they do." Melanie giggled. "And knit nice little woolly covers for them."

Katrin glanced over, and Della could see the hurt in her eyes. Some of the girls shuffled their feet uncomfortably, but no one spoke. *You are so mean,* Della yelled, although no one heard her, because the words never left her head.

"I'm going to the library," Della murmured, hoping Katrin might follow her. Then she could say something nice to make up for Melanie's meanness.

"Wait. Why?" Anna questioned. "It's recess."

"There's a book I want to look at that might help me with the history homework."

"You don't know what you're going to present yet?" Sophie said in astonishment.

"Well, I'm working on it."

"But history is next," Anna reminded her. "It's right after recess."

"I know. That's why I've got to look at this book."

"You mean *The Book of Spells*, I bet," Melanie said, "because it has medieval enchantments and stuff on Witch Dupree in there."

"I need some inspiration." Della sighed, finding it hard to explain that she wanted to discover a special connection with Witch Dupree, something that would make her presentation stand out. "But I've no idea what I should do."

"Well, I pretended I was writing a letter to one of my friends," Sophie said. "Telling them how I go out at night to gather ingredients for my spells so no one sees me and gets suspicious."

"Oh, that's good. Mine's a diary entry," Samantha Perkins said. "I wrote about how I have to do magic in secret, and how lonely I feel being a witch."

"You don't know Della Dupree was lonely," Melanie butted in.

"I can imagine," Samantha said. "Which is what Miss Barlow told us to do."

"Anyway, Miss Dickenson won't let you take that book out," Cassie remarked. "We tried. Only year twelve girls can look at it."

"Well, I'm still going to the library," Della said. "Because either way I've got to present something, and at least I can concentrate there."

The library was quiet, and a number of girls looked up in irritation as Della walked over to the checkout desk, her shoes squeaking noisily on the floor.

"Sorry," she mouthed to the room.

"Della, how nice to see you," Miss Dickenson the librarian said, leaning across the desk. "How's Pickle doing?" They often discussed pets during library class.

"Still not eating much. I left him at home today." Smiling at Miss Dickenson, Della inquired, "And how's your cat doing? Has she had kittens yet?"

"Oh, aren't you sweet to ask. Two days ago. Seven of them, and the most adorable bundles of fur you've ever seen." Miss Dickenson whipped out her phone and started scrolling through it, holding it out so Della could see the pictures.

"They are adorable," Della agreed, wondering how many photos there were. Recess was only twenty minutes. After about the seventy-fifth picture Della said, "Miss Dickenson, do you think I might have a quick look at *The Book of Spells*? I'm doing a project on Della Dupree for history, and I'm a bit stuck." She put on her most beseeching face. "It's so hard being named after the most famous witch in history, and I know Miss Barlow thinks my presentation should be brilliant." Della gave a dramatic sigh.

Glancing around the room, Miss Dickenson murmured, "Well, I really shouldn't. And you can't take it out of the library, Della. But if it's just a quick peek, and you're very careful . . ."

"Oh, Miss Dickenson, you're the best! I'm just looking for some inspiration. I really won't be long." Della glanced at the clock. "I can't be long." It was already 10:40. She only had ten minutes to spare.

"Go and sit over there." Miss Dickenson nodded at an old oak table in the corner. She handed Della a pair of thin white gloves. "And you must put these on before you handle it."

For some reason Della couldn't explain, her heart was racing extra hard as Miss Dickenson put down a smallish, leather-bound book. She was expecting something big and engraved, but from the outside this was about the plainest book Della had ever seen. There wasn't even a title on the cracked brown cover. Pulling on the gloves (which she was glad to have, because her hands had started to sweat), Della waited for Miss Dickenson to leave, and then very carefully she opened it.

Della blinked as a cloud of glittery dust rose off the first page, swirling around her in a mist. There was a strong smell of spices and burnt caramel, mingled with the fizzy scent of magic that made her want to sneeze. Lute music played faintly, seeming to come from the pages of the book, and Della stared at the spiky handwriting, which had faded to the color of chestnuts. She tried to read, but it was as if she couldn't absorb the words, and a strange but powerful thought suddenly occurred to her. Books were all very well, but if she could talk to Della Dupree, if she could see what things were like back then and hear about being a witch in Della's own words, she could give an amazing presentation. "That's what I have to do," Della whispered, getting to her feet. Her head felt heavy and full of treacle as she left the library. She sensed Miss Dickenson calling after her, but she sounded so far off and faint, Della wasn't sure.

Walking directly to the fortune-telling lab, Della marched over and opened up the cabinet that held the time-travel amulets. Even though she knew she would get into a great deal of trouble if anyone discovered what she was doing, for some reason this didn't bother her. With an unusual display of confidence, Della took out one of the necklaces and slipped it on. They were all programmed to return the girls to the exact time and place of their leaving, but you had to be clear about where you wanted to go.

The chain was chunky but featherlight, being made out of moon gold, and hanging from the center was the fossilized dragon's eye, a deep amber color flecked with green and copper streaks. Holding the fossil in her hands, Della stared into its center. She could hear words coming out of her mouth, although they didn't seem to be linked to her thoughts.

"Twelve twenty-three, twelve twenty-three, Ruthersfield was founded by Witch Dupree."

The dragon's eye started to glow, and a buzzing in Della's head got louder, as if a swarm of bees had nested in there. A wind picked her up, and for a moment she felt like she was being sucked inside a vacuum. Cold air blew around her, and the buzzing turned into a gushing, swirling roar. Della covered her ears and shut her eyes, and when the noise finally stopped, she lay perfectly still, feeling twigs press against her check and smelling the damp scent of earth after a rainfall. A bird cawed, and Della gingerly opened her eyes, realizing that she was lying on the floor of a forest.

Chapter Four

. . . .

A Show of Magic

WHAT ON EARTH HAVE I DONE?" DELLA WHISPERED, SIT-
ting up and pulling a leaf out of her hair. For a
moment her thoughts were so jumbled up she couldn't
work out what had just happened. She remembered
opening *The Book of Spells* and then thinking how much
better it would be to try to talk to Witch Dupree herself, to go back in time and see what life was like. But
the fact that she'd actually gone and done it? Taken a
travel amulet from the lab and transported herself back
to 1223? Della shook her head and groaned. This was
not at all the sort of thing she usually did. Daring and
risky belonged to the other Della Dupree.

"Except I did do it," Della whispered, thinking that maybe there was some strange ancient magic stuck in the book that had made her react that way. Rubbing the blurriness from her eyes, she looked around. The forest was so dense with trees, not much light could come through, and Della had no intention of staying here very long. She tried to remember what Ms. Randal had taught them to say on the return journey. *Ruthersfield now!* That was it. A soft rustle sent her hand grasping for the amulet. What if there were wolves prowling about? The last thing she wanted was to meet one. Deciding she had seen enough to write about (how dark and scary medieval woods were), Della opened her mouth to speak. But just as she was about to say the return command, she heard what sounded like sobbing coming from a nearby thicket. Human sobbing. Creeping closer, Della saw a wooden pail on the ground, half-full of blackberries.

"Hello?" Della called out softly. The crying stopped, and there was a scuffling noise. Peering into the bushes, Della saw a frightened pair of eyes staring back at her through the leaves. "Are you okay?" she whispered. There was still no answer. "You can come out. I won't hurt you."

After a minute or two the sobbing started up again, great heaving sobs that sounded like whoever was in there was having trouble breathing.

"All right, I'm coming in, because you clearly need help."

"No, don't," a small voice gasped. "You mustn't. You'll tell on me."

"I promise I won't," Della said, wondering what on earth could be the matter. "I just want to help."

There was a rather long silence and then the sound of branches snapping as a strange green creature crawled out of the bushes. The creature stood up, and Della stared in surprise, because it wasn't some sort of extinct medieval beast. It was a little girl. A little green girl with green braids and green skin; even her clothes were the same exact mottled shade of green as the blackberry thicket she'd been hiding in. The only things that weren't green were her eyes, a pale, watery blue and so full of fear that Della took a step back, not wanting to frighten the girl further.

"It's all right. I'm a friend," Della murmured. "Don't be scared."

The girl pointed a shaky finger at Della's clothes, and glancing down, Della saw that she was still in her school uniform. The gold-trimmed purple jacket and purple pleated skirt must have looked as strange to this girl as her greenness did to Della.

"It's what we wear in my village," Della said, deciding that this was not the time to try to explain where she had come from and why she was dressed this way.

"You're not from around here?" The girl's voice was so soft, Della had to strain to hear.

"I'm not, no."

Picking up the pail, the girl hugged it to her chest. She didn't take her eyes off Della as she reached into the bucket and popped a blackberry into her mouth. Almost immediately her skin and clothes began to turn purple, a deep, dark purple like the berry she was eating. Staring at her arm, the girl dropped the pail on the ground, spilling out the fruit. "No, no, no!" she wailed, starting to cry again, and where her tears hit the ground, delicate purple violets sprouted up. The girl screamed, crushing the violets with her feet and sending a heady floral fragrance into the air. "What's happening?" she sobbed.

"Oh, I think I understand," Della said in relief. "I thought you had some weird disease, but you don't." A cloud of purple butterflies flew out of the girl's tunic pockets, and Della smiled. "It looks like you've got the gift, that's all. This is a good thing," she added.

"Gift?"

"Of magic," Della explained. "You're a witch."

"NO!" The girl curled up on the ground, covering her head with her arms. "Don't say that. Don't say that ever again. I'm not a witch. I can't be."

"How old are you?" Della crouched beside the girl. "Is this the first time something like this has happened?"

The girl nodded, continuing to cry. There was a thick carpet of violets around them now, and the scent was intoxicating. "This is my seventh year."

"That's about the age magic shows up. I was five," Della said, putting a gentle hand on the girl's back.

"You're a witch?"

"I changed my bathwater into lime jelly and blew hundreds of green bubbles into the air. One of them was so big I floated out of the tub on it. Magic often begins by turning things different colors."

"I don't want to be a different color," the girl wept. "My parents will send me away. They'll have me locked up in the castle."

"I'm sure they won't," Della said. "I'll come and explain to them. Make them understand that being a witch is a wonderful thing. Okay, sometimes it's a bit stressful," Della added, thinking about her history project, "but most of the time it's great."

"No it's not." The girl shook her head vigorously. Lowering her voice, she glanced around and said, "Last harvest there was a witch in Pig Hollow who put a hex on the wheat crop so it withered and died, and the village didn't have any food for the winter. And there was a witch in Deckle Mead who turned all the cows into mice. And," the girl continued without taking a breath, "one in Little Shamlington who gave Lord Middlebury donkey ears. Witches are evil," she finished with a shudder. "I don't want to be one."

Della couldn't help thinking that maybe these witches were driven to do such terrible things because everyone hated them so much. And how awful to try to keep your magic hidden so no one knew you had the gift. Reading about the Middle Ages was quite different from actually being here. This was not a place she wanted to spend any more time in than she had to. "Well, I agree that doesn't sound too good. But most witches aren't like that," Della insisted.

"Yes they are. They're evil and malicious. That's what mama says."

"You don't look evil or malicious to me."

"I would never hurt anyone." The girl looked up at Della out of enormous, frightened eyes.

"And see these beautiful violets you made? How can magic be so terrible if it makes something this pretty?" This made the girl smile, and she wiped a hand across her damp cheeks. "What's your name?" Della asked.

"Mary."

"Well, I'm Della." Continuing to rub circles on the girl's back, Della tried to remember what Ms. Pringle, her year one teacher, had taught them about regulating their magic. "Can you take some deep, slow breaths for me, Mary?" she said. "It will help get rid of the purple." Mary did what Della instructed, and immediately the color started to drain away from her skin and clothes, and her hair turned a pretty copper color. "Wow, it actually worked!" Della said, feeling quite pleased with herself. "Magic can be very temperamental in the beginning," she explained. "Breathing like this will help you control it." The girls sat quietly for a few more minutes until Della said, "Now let's get these berries picked up so you can take them home to your mum." Because until Mary went home, Della couldn't exactly disappear back to Ruthersfield.

"Wait, someone's coming," Mary whispered, a look of panic sweeping over her face.

Della listened, and sure enough, footsteps could be heard crunching through the forest, accompanied by the tinkling sound of bells. Swiftly she pulled her wand out of her pocket and swept it over her uniform. "Changeotimeo," Della murmured, her smart Ruthersfield jacket and skirt becoming a long, loose-fitting dress with a purple cape over it. She touched a hand to her head and was pleased to discover what felt like a rather complicated set of braids wound around it instead of her usual wispy hair hanging down. And even though this wasn't a good time for such a thought,

Della couldn't help wishing she had a mirror handy.

Mary opened her mouth to say something, but Della put a finger to her lips, waving a hand around to disperse the faint purple smoke left over from the spell. She could see a man bounding toward them, wearing a red-and-green jester hat, scarlet tunic, and what looked like a pair of brown woven tights. It was more of a skip than a bound, and at the sight of Della and Mary he stopped, bowing low at the waist and making a sweeping curly gesture with his arm.

"Good day, my fair maidens." The man tilted his head up and sniffed, cutting his eyes toward Della. There was a sweet smell of magic still lingering in the air, like slightly burnt toffee, and Della moved a few steps away, hoping he didn't recognize it. She could feel her heart pounding and wished the man would stop staring at her in that slightly unnerving way, although when he spoke, his voice was all bubbly and friendly.

"Tom Foolery at your service, but it would be my pleasure if you called me Tom." He darted over toward Mary and put his face up close to hers. "Someone has been crying, I see. And on such a pretty day as this."

"Her berries spilled," Della said quickly, wondering who this strange person was, and rather liking being called a "fair maiden."

The man looked as if he might be about to cry. He

raised a hand in front of his face and drew it upward, turning the sad look into a smile. Then he shook his head, jiggling the bells on the ends of his floppy hat, and turned a swift somersault over the ground.

Mary laughed, and Della couldn't help joining in. He was so ridiculously silly it was impossible not to.

"I am employed by Lord Hepworth," Tom said.

"In the castle," Mary explained, which didn't add much clarity to the conversation for Della. "He performs in the village sometimes. On feast days."

"That's nice," Della said, feeling like she was in the middle of a bad dream and desperately wanting to wake up.

Tom Foolery started to dance around the girls, waving his hands in the air and pulling all kinds of ridiculous faces that made Mary giggle and Della want to run away. Clearly nobody had explained to Tom Foolery about personal space. He danced up to Mary and, with a flourish, pulled a coin out of her ear.

"Now you see it," Tom Foolery said, closing his hand around the coin. "And now you don't." Mary giggled in delight as Tom Foolery peeled back his fingers to show them that the coin had disappeared. "Oh where did it go?" he said, skipping over to Della. Standing far too close, he fluttered his hands in front of her face, and once again Della felt he was scrutinizing her, as if he could sense that she wasn't what she seemed. She caught a flash of suspicion in his gaze as he reached up and tugged a coin out of her braid. "Here it is!" the jester said. Mary laughed, and Tom Foolery smiled back. "Happy noise. Oh joy of joys. And now I must be on my way. I'm off to Deckle Mead to cheer up Lord Hepworth's cousin. He has been feeling melancholy and has retired to his bed." Giving them one last bow and another fancy wave, he bounded off, much to Della's relief. That is until she put her hand up to her neck and started to pat about, more and more frantically. "It's gone." Della panicked, shaking her cloak and peering down the front of her gown. "It was here a second ago, and now it's gone." She gave a low, hysterical wail. "And it can't break. The chain is moon gold."

Mary stared at Della. "What's gone?"

"My necklace." Della spun in circles, searching the ground just in case it had fallen off. "The one I was wearing. That Tom person took it. I knew he was weird. We have to go after him." She ran a few feet ahead, but the forest was thick with trees, and there was no sign of the jester at all. Of course he had disappeared.

"He's good at making things vanish," Mary said. "That's one of his tricks."

"That's not a trick—that's stealing," Della said. "Where on earth is Deckle Mead? I have to find him."

"I'm not sure." Mary shrugged. "He'll be back in a day or two, though. He never stays away from the castle for long."

"Oh, this is worse than a nightmare, and I don't know what to do." Della's stomach cramped, and her legs went all wobbly. Feeling sick and dizzy, she collapsed on the ground. She patted her neck again. But the time-travel amulet definitely wasn't there.

Chapter Five

....

Return to Potts Bottom

I CAN'T GO HOME," DELLA WHISPERED, PULLING HER legs up and wrapping her arms around her knees. "Not without my necklace." She dropped her head down, realizing she was going to have to go to the castle and confront that horrible jester. Which seemed almost as distressing as being stuck here.

"I can't go home either," Mary cried. "The berries won't stay still. Mama will be so cross." Della looked up, watching Mary pick a blackberry off the ground and drop it into the pail. But immediately the berry floated out, hovering in the air until a bird swooped past and ate it. "I feel so strange," Mary wailed, starting to turn purple again. "Like I have an inside-out itch I can't scratch."

"Oh, Mary, that's just your magic," Della said, hating to see the little girl so upset. "Deep breaths, remember. Staying calm is the key. Here, you sit still," Della instructed. "I'll get the berries." She scrambled to her feet and, trying not to step on them, gathered all the unsquished blackberries back in the pail. "There, now your mother won't be mad, and you'll probably have enough for a pie."

Mary's lip trembled. "My parents can't know I'm a witch, Della. Nor can my brothers. It will break their hearts. As soon as they find out, I'll get sent away."

"I really can't believe they'd do that," Della said, remembering how excited her own parents had been when they realized she had inherited the magic gene, throwing her a party and telling everyone in Potts Bottom, making her feel like being a witch was the most wonderful thing in the whole world.

"It happened to a girl in our village," Mary whispered. "One day she flew out of the window on a wooden spoon, and her parents were so worried she had put a hex on them both that they told Lord Hepworth and had her locked up. Can't I stay with you?" Mary said, looking terrified.

"Oh, Mary, I don't have anywhere to stay. I can't

go home, remember. Not without my necklace." The knot of worry tightened in Della's stomach, and she touched a hand to her neck again, finding it impossible to believe the dragon's eye had gone.

"Will you come home with me then?" Mary pleaded, reminding Della of Pickle. She had the same helpless look the baby duckling had had when Della found him. "Just for tonight. You help keep my magic inside."

The light was growing dim, and Della realized that she was actually going to have to stay here, at least until she had got her travel amulet back from that Tom Foolery person. If she could get it back at all. But that was too scary to think about. So scary that Della's mind switched off at the mere thought of such a thing, her brain going fuzzy and a crackly noise buzzing in her ears.

"All right, I'll take you home," Della said, not wanting to abandon Mary, and relieved to have somewhere to go. Spending the night in a medieval forest was not an option she cared to consider. She reached for Mary's hand and gave it a squeeze, which seemed to calm Mary down and also helped remind Della that she wasn't completely alone out here. "It's going to be fine," Della murmured, wishing she could actually believe this.

"Where do you live?" Della asked as Mary led her

through the forest. The trees were tall, and Della could tell from the acorns scattered across the ground that most of them were oaks.

"Potts Bottom. It's not far from here."

"Oh, you do!" Just hearing the name made Della feel closer to home. At least she had ended up in the right place, which, with any luck, meant she had ended up in the right year as well. And if that was the case, Della reasoned, remembering why she had come back here to begin with, then Witch Dupree should be somewhere close by. All she had to do was find her and explain what had happened. And maybe, Della thought hopefully, Witch Dupree could help her get home again. Maybe she even had a travel amulet hanging about that Della could borrow, so she wouldn't have to confront that horrible creepy jester.

"Twelve twenty-three, twelve twenty-three, Ruthersfield was founded by Witch Dupree." Della hadn't realized she was speaking out loud until Mary yanked her to a stop.

"You can't say that word." Mary mouthed "witch." "Ever. Even talk of such things is dangerous."

"I'm sorry. I didn't mean to." Della glanced around as they started to walk again. "But have you heard of Della Dupree?" she whispered, being careful not to use the word "witch."

"No." Mary shook her head. "You're the only Della I know."

"Are you sure there's not another Della in Potts Bottom?"

"I haven't heard of anyone by that name. Is she a friend of yours?"

"I thought she might be able to help me," Della sighed. "I've heard great things about her."

"She could live in Deckle Mead or Pig Hollow," Mary suggested. "There are other villages around here."

"Maybe. I don't know." Della wished she had done a little more research on Witch Dupree. Had she actually lived in Potts Bottom? Della couldn't remember. "And there's no school called Ruthersfield nearby?" she asked hopefully.

"There's no school at all." Mary laughed. "What would we be wanting one of those for? Too much to do, with harvesting and planting and helping out with the spinning and weaving and taking care of the animals."

"So no one goes to school?"

"Master Ivan, Lord Hepworth's son, has a tutor. And there are some that can read and write."

The girls walked on in silence for a bit, and Della noticed that the wood was getting lighter. The trees weren't so dense, and they had joined a well-traveled path that finally led out to open land, where a number of huts were gathered. The huts appeared to be made out of sticks and mud with thatched roofs of straw. Smoke streamed out of holes in the roofs instead of chimneys, and a thin, bluish haze hung over the settlement. A pair of goats wandered past them, and Della could see chickens pecking in the earth for food. Beyond the settlement were open fields, some with cows and sheep grazing on them and others that looked like they had been planted in long, distinct strips. Children ran up and down among the crops, waving their arms about.

"What are they doing?" Della whispered to Mary, feeling like she had stumbled upon a movie set.

"Scaring the birds away." Mary gave Della a strange look that seemed to imply she should know this.

"Wait. Where exactly are we?" Della said, staring at the hill in front of them. It looked remarkably like Clackton Ridge, the place Della's class had flown to on a field trip a few weeks ago. Except that now there was a castle standing on the grassy mound where they had picnicked.

"Potts Bottom, of course."

"Are you sure?" Della turned toward a banging noise. She saw a blacksmith hammering a piece of iron over a fire. Sparks flew into the air, and Della shut her eyes for a minute, picturing the Potts Bottom she had just left, with its brick houses and cobbled streets and girls whizzing about on broomsticks. It was hard to believe the two places were connected. Surprisingly, there was a familiar scent of yeasty baking, mingling with the smell of woodsmoke, and for a moment Della half expected to see Poppy's bakery. But of course there was no little shop sitting by the canal, because the canal hadn't been built yet. The smell, Della realized, came from one of the huts they were walking past, and her stomach rumbled in response. She hadn't eaten since breakfast and would have given anything for one of Poppy's sticky-topped lemon muffins. Della watched a woman walk out with a loaf of bread and (more surprisingly) two others walk in with covered bowls. She didn't mean to stare quite so hard until Mary nudged her. "Haven't you seen a baker's before?"

"What are they taking inside?" Della asked, her mouth watering.

"Dough," Mary said. "The oven is for the whole village." She gave Della another strange look, as if this was more information she should know.

"It's very different where I come from," Della explained. "Very different."

"I think I'd like to live in your country," Mary said, touching a hand to her cheek. "Am I changing color again?" she whispered. "My skin is tingling."

"Just breathe slowly," Della murmured, taking the

bucket from Mary in case she sent it floating away with her magic. "You're fine."

"I'm so hot," Mary said, leading Della over to a well in the center of the settlement. She cranked a handle round and pulled up a pail filled with water. Dipping her hands in, Mary splashed some on her face. "My parents cannot find out."

"I really think we should tell them," Della whispered. "I'm sure they'll understand. I can explain about all the amazing things wit—" She clapped a hand against her mouth, remembering just in time.

Luckily, there seemed to be some sort of commotion going on, so no one was looking at the girls. "News," a young boy yelled, racing through the village. He stopped near the well and cupped his hands around his mouth. "News," he shouted again. "A witch was discovered in Little Shamlington, flying on the back of a pig. They say she turned all the milk sour before leaving."

Hut doors opened, and villagers streamed outside. Some looked up in the air as if expecting to see a pig flying over.

"Oh my stars," a woman gasped, grabbing the arm of her neighbor. Her face trembled with the horror and excitement of such news. "A pig, indeed!"

"Okay, I think you're right," Della whispered. "We won't say anything to your parents."

Chapter Six

....

A Nasty Pottage and a Very Tasty Spell

MARY'S HUT WAS LIKE MOST OF THE OTHERS, WITH two square holes cut in the wall for windows, but no glass covering them, just shutters to keep out the dust and noise. Mary pushed open the wooden door, and immediately Della's eyes smarted from the smoke. An open fire smoldered in the center of the room, and hanging above it from an iron hook dangled a heavy cast-iron pot, remarkably similar to an antique cauldron. A woman was leaning over the pot, stirring the contents around with a long wooden spoon.

"Who's this then?" she said, eyeing Della coldly.

"Della," Mary said. "She helped me pick up my berries when I spilled them."

"Hope you got the dust off." Mary's mother gave Della a curt nod. "Where are you from?"

"Potts Bottom," Della said without thinking.

Mary's mother frowned. "I've not seen you around these parts before."

"I — I mean I was on my way to Potts Bottom," Della said, stumbling over her words.

"Looking for work, no doubt."

Even though Della was small for her size, back here she felt surprisingly tall. She remembered reading that people were much shorter in medieval times due to a poor diet, so maybe she looked old enough to be job hunting. Or maybe, Della decided, thinking about Mary's reaction from earlier, it was perfectly normal for kids to have jobs and be wandering about the countryside.

"Well, there's nothing here," Mary's mother continued, sprinkling a dried leaf of some sort into the pot. "You might have luck at the castle, though. They're often looking for help."

"They are?" Della said, realizing this was the perfect excuse she needed. All she had to do was pretend she was looking for work, track down Tom Foolery, and convince him to be a nice, kind jester and give her the necklace back. Of course it wasn't going to be that easy, and the thought of actually doing it made Della groan softly.

"Are you feeling all right, child?" Mary's mother inquired.

"Just tired," Della said. Which happened to be true. She was also frightened and homesick, and this was the last place on earth she wanted to be right now. Her eyes stung from the smoke, and Della hoped she wouldn't start crying. But at least she had a plan. Then she'd be out of this nightmare and back in the fortune-telling lab, and nobody (thankfully) would have missed her.

"Can Della stay tonight?" Mary asked.

"Only if you have room," Della added, glancing around the hut and wondering where she was supposed to sleep. There was a strong smell of animal that seemed to be coming from the two goats curled up in a corner.

"That's Crabapple and Bay Leaf," Mary said, as if it were perfectly normal to have goats in the house.

Mary's mother put down the stirring spoon and folded her arms. "There's not much to eat, so don't go expecting a full belly."

"I'm not very hungry," Della said, feeling slightly nauseous from the sour smell coming out of the pot. And she lost her appetite completely as the door banged open, letting in the ripe stench of sweat and unwashed bodies along with three rather ogrelike men. On closer inspection, two were more boys than men, and Della guessed they had doused their heads in the well, because water dripped from their hair onto the floor.

"Who's this then?" the oldest man grunted, stamping his boots and nodding at Della. She nodded back, too intimidated to speak.

"Girl's looking for work at the castle," Mary's mother explained.

"And she helped me in the woods," Mary said. "I fell over and spilled all my berries. Della was kind to me and made sure I wasn't hurt."

The man mumbled a greeting. Although no one introduced him, Della guessed he was Mary's father, and the two boys had to be her brothers.

Immediately Mary's mother started serving the vile-smelling stew into bowls. The family sat on two hard benches; Della squeezed onto one end beside Mary, trying not to think about her own family mealtimes, the warm cozy chaos with Robbie refusing to touch his broccoli and everyone chattering about their day. Here there was no conversation, and Della stared into her bowl, wondering what on earth she was eating, or trying to eat. It was almost impossible to swallow the watery mess with bits of gray, stringy stuff floating in it, and Della couldn't believe how quickly the others slurped theirs down.

"Did you hear about that witch in Little Shamlington?" one of the boys said. "Flying on a pig."

"They'll catch her," the other boy continued. "Before she does any more harm. Lord Hepworth's sent some of his knights to join in the hunt."

"Wicked things," Mary's mother murmured. "Get them young before they start casting their evil spells everywhere."

Della's heart raced. How could they be so ignorant? She should say something, but her mouth was dry, and she could feel Mary shaking beside her.

"Poor girl's terrified," one of the boys said, nodding at his sister.

"Wipe the bowls and stop fretting," Mary's mother muttered. "And close the shutters, Mary, just in case."

"If any witch flies through the window, I'll swat her with the broom and pitch her on the fire," one of the boys bragged. Della gasped, and Mary bolted from the table.

"I'll help too," Della croaked, standing up rather shakily. Partly because she thought she might suffocate from the smell, but mainly because she couldn't stand listening to such awful talk.

Taking the bowls from the table, Della looked around to ask Mary what they did with them, but the girl seemed to have vanished. It wasn't a big hut, and trying not to draw attention to Mary's disappearance, Della padded across the room. Thankfully, the rest of the family was too absorbed in their conversation to notice. Not wanting to call out Mary's name, Della peered into the gloom. A horrible thought suddenly occurred to her. What if Mary had managed to turn invisible? Untrained magic could do all sorts of strange things, and Della remembered hearing about a four-year-old who kept going in and out of focus when she first got the gift.

There was a rustling near the goats, and at first Della thought a third animal had wandered inside to join them. It looked to be the same mottled color, but on closer inspection Della saw that the small creature tucked between Crabapple and Bay Leaf was actually Mary. Her skin and tunic mimicked the identical brown and cream of Bay Leaf's hair, and it dawned on Della that Mary's magic was acting as camouflage, helping her blend in with her surroundings. Perhaps it was a protection technique, nature's way of shielding Mary from her magic being discovered? This would have been a fascinating thing to think about if Della were back at Ruthersfield, but right now not being hit with a broom and tossed on the fire seemed rather more pressing.

"Deep, slow breaths," Della said, glancing over at the table. Luckily, none of the family appeared to be the least bit interested in the girls. "Just relax," Della murmured. "Draw your—" She was about to say "magic" but remembered just in time. "Draw your energy into your belly. Keep it tucked up inside," she whispered, sounding just like Ms. Pringle. This made Mary giggle, and she pressed her hands over her mouth. But as soon as she began to practice her breathing, Della could see the color fading fast, and it wasn't long before Mary was back to normal.

Washing the dishes, Della discovered, involved wiping them out with a bit of rag and putting them back on the shelf, which made her miss the squabbles she and her brothers always had about whose turn it was to load the dishwasher. It got more and more difficult to see as the light faded outside, and even the low flicker of a candle didn't offer much in the way of illumination. There was no entertainment after supper, and when it got too dark to see each other clearly, the family crawled onto straw pallets, removing the outer layer of their clothes but not bothering to wash, or brush their teeth or put on pajamas. Della lay down beside Mary, who lay beside the goats, and before long the sound of snoring filled the hut. But Della was far too hungry and cold to sleep, and the few sips of gruel she'd choked down had left a sour, horrible taste in her mouth.

It was difficult to breathe because of the smoke and the smells, and a powerful, aching homesickness overtook Della. She wanted so much to be back on Button Street, with her brothers and her mum and dad, eating her mum's lasagna. She missed Pickle and Flutter and the bats, and the warm weight of Robbie curled up in her lap for a story. And she wanted a hot bath full of Amazing Dreams Bath Powder and to be tucked up in her own bed with her phoenix-feather pillow. The ache inside Della grew so strong that she found herself gripping her magic wand, buried deep in the pocket of the strange dress she now wore, desperate for a small taste of home. Della's mouth watered as she imagined the flavors of noodles and cheese and meat sauce. Being as quiet as she could, she stood up, checking that the wooden shutters were fastened. Then, waving her wand in the darkness, Della whispered, "Slumberoco," a spell the girls often used at sleepovers. A flash of sparkles shot into the air, forming a lamb-shaped cloud that glowed luminous pale silver. The cloud floated around the room, and as it passed over the pallets where Mary's brothers and parents slept, drifts of silver sparkles floated down on them. Continuing to glow, the lamb cloud settled above the fireplace, giving off a gentle moonlit radiance.

Crouching beside the fire, Della waved her wand over the cooking pot. "Italiomama," she whispered, suddenly glad that her strength was in practical magic. Who cared if she didn't get As on her math quizzes? Right now this was much more useful. Immediately the most delicious smells started wafting into the air. Practicing the witch survival skills they had learned in outdoor magic class, Della transformed her wand into a spoon. (She also knew how to turn it into a toothpick, a pair of tweezers, and scissors.) Her stomach rumbled rather loudly as she dipped the spoon into the pot, ladling up a gooey cheesy mouthful of lasagna.

"Oh that's good," Della sighed, dipping her spoon in again and again. It didn't taste exactly like her mother's (slightly heavy on the garlic), but it was incredibly delicious. And exactly what Della needed. In fact, she was so busy eating, she didn't hear footsteps padding across the earthen floor.

"What are you doing?" Mary whispered, startling Della so she dropped her spoon.

"Mary! You scared me. You shouldn't creep up on people like that."

"But what are you doing?" Mary whispered again. "Why aren't you sleeping? And what's that?" She was pointing at the silvery lamb cloud hanging above the fire.

"Okay, no need to panic, because your family is sound asleep. I've put them under a spell."

Mary scrambled backward, staring at Della.

"No, listen," Della said, realizing Mary was actually scared. "It's not like that. I'm not evil. I miss my family, and this is magic to make me feel better." Tears clouded her eyes, and Della sniffed, wiping her hands across her face. "I just want to go home," she confessed, "but I knew if your family saw me doing magic they would . . ." Della stopped and gave a shudder, not exactly sure what Mary's family would do, except whatever it was it wouldn't be good.

"Will they wake up again?" Mary said, still eyeing Della nervously.

"In the morning, as usual. This will actually make them feel very well rested. Take away some of their aches and pains. It's a good spell."

"And it came from the lamb cloud?"

"It did." Della managed a watery smile. "This is a wonderful enchantment. It gives light as well as sleep."

"And what's in the pot?" Mary asked, inching closer to the fire again.

"Lasagna. Made by a traditional Italian grandmother, or that's what the spell claims."

"Lasagna? Is that like pottage?"

"Is pottage what we had for supper?"

"Yes. We have it most days."

"Then no. It definitely isn't like pottage." Della

picked up her wand spoon and dipped it into the pot. "Try some, Mary."

"I don't think so."

"Come on. It won't hurt you. It's not poisonous."

Mary's eyes were round with fear. "But you're a witch."

"So are you."

"I don't want to be."

"Well, try this and you might change your mind." Della held out the spoon, and Mary shuffled closer. When she was near enough to reach, she leaned forward and took a tiny taste.

"Oh my." Mary opened her mouth wide, finishing off the whole spoonful. "Like warm heaven," she whispered. "I've never had anything like it."

"Finish it," Della said. "Go on. I've had plenty."

Mary didn't need any coaxing, and while Della watched, she set about scraping the pot clean. When there was nothing left but a crusty edge, Mary gave a soft burp and said, "Are there good witches and bad witches, Della?"

"Just like there are good people and bad people," Della answered. "But most witches are good, Mary."

"Why doesn't everybody think that?"

"I don't know," Della replied, shaking her head. She was quiet for a minute. "I really don't know."

Chapter Seven

························

Things Do Not Improve

DELLA WOKE TO ONE OF THE GOATS TRAMPLING OVER her legs. Her throat was sore from breathing in smoke, but the shutters had been flung open, and light streamed into the hut. She could see Mary hooking a basket over her arm. The men had all gone, and Mary's mother was already sitting at a spinning wheel in a corner of the hut.

"Do you want to collect eggs?" Mary asked, smiling at Della.

Della nodded. She patted her knotty tangle of braids, wishing she had a brush.

"There's a heel of bread you can have," Mary's

mother called out gruffly. "But no more pottage. I'm saving what's left for the boys when they come back from the fields."

"That's quite okay," Della said quickly. "Bread is fine." And even though it tasted coarse and had the texture of a brick, smeared with honey and berries it wasn't a bad breakfast.

Outside, Della blinked in the sharp light. A stream of villagers hurried past lugging pails of water from the well. Some of them threw Della curious glances, and she tried to look natural, as if she belonged here. Next door to the hut stood a small shelter filled with hay.

"The chickens love to lay eggs in here," Mary said, skipping into the shed. She rooted around in a pile of hay and pulled out a pretty, speckled egg, balancing it on her palm for Della to see. "Still warm." The egg suddenly spun around on Mary's hand, floated into the air, and sailed out of the shack.

"Quick, get it!" Della cried, but Mary had frozen in a panic, and as Della charged outside, she watched the egg zoom through the air, splattering against the side of a tree.

"Hey, who's throwing eggs?" a woman yelled fiercely, looking around to see where it had come from.

Della ducked back into the shed to find Mary

crouched on the floor. "It's all right, Mary. She doesn't know what happened. She didn't see."

"I'm going to get caught," Mary whispered. "I'll get found out and taken away."

"No you won't." Della knelt beside her. "And your magic will start to calm down soon, I promise."

Mary stared at her hands as if they might betray her again. After a few minutes she got up and very carefully filled the basket with eggs. " Please don't go to the castle just yet, Della. At least come to the woods to help me get sticks." Her voice shook a little. "I don't want to be by myself."

"Of course I'll come," Della said, thinking again how much Mary reminded her of Pickle. And how much she wanted to go home.

Mary's mother gave them a cloth sack to fill with kindling, the small twigs and bits of wood that were light enough for Mary to carry. Nodding at Della, she said crisply, "I wish you well looking for work," which Della took to mean "Please don't come back here again."

"Thank you for your hospitality," Della said, slipping her hand into her pocket and discovering that she didn't have her magic wand. She remembered changing it back from a spoon last night and wiping it clean on the washrag, but after that . . . Della frowned.

It had to be on the floor where she'd been sitting. Turning to the center of the room, she saw Mary's mother toss a handful of sticks on the fire, and Della knew, as soon as the smell of burning treacle hit the air, what had happened. It was a powerful scent, sweet and spicy, like overcooked gingerbread. Silver sparks fizzed and popped in the flames, and a sick dread filled Della as she watched a long, sticklike shape glowing purple.

"Heaven above." Mary's mother wrinkled up her nose. "What on earth is that wood? It reeks of scorched honey."

Della stared at the fire, a hot queasiness spreading over her. How could she have been so careless? There was no mistaking the smell of burning magic.

Mary looked at Della, and Della nodded dumbly. Now she had no wand to help her survive, as well as no way of getting home.

"Well, be off with you then," Mary's mother said, shooing them both outside. "And don't go bringing me back any more of that wood, Mary. It's making my head ache with the smell."

Della knew she was putting one foot in front of the other, but it was as if she were on autopilot. Her body was moving, but her mind was still back in the hut, trying to absorb the fact that she had just watched her magic wand go up in flames.

"Is this a calamity?" Mary whispered, taking Della's hand.

"Well, I can't make any more lasagna, so I suppose it's a bit of a calamity," Della said, trying to stay calm in front of Mary. What she wanted to do was bang her head against a tree for being so stupid.

"What will you do now?"

"I'll help you collect firewood, and then I'm going to have to get my necklace back. So I can go home."

"What will I do?" Mary whispered as the girls stepped into the wood.

"Just keep doing what I've taught you." Della could hear how worried Mary sounded, and wanting to give her hope, she added, "Look, Mary, I don't think it's going to be too long before people realize that— that girls like us aren't as terrible as everyone seems to think." She didn't want to say more, because Ms. Randal was always drumming into them how important it was when you visited the past to be there as an observer, and not to talk about the future. "Now let's get this bag filled for you."

The girls walked around the wood, stuffing the cloth sack with twigs. There was something calming about it, the crunch of dry leaves underfoot and the chirping of birds. Occasionally a rabbit would hop past, and at one point Della found herself nose to nose with a deer.

But this all changed as the sound of a horn cut through the peace, and somewhere in the distance came the rumble of hooves.

"It's Lord Hepworth." Mary panicked. "I don't like it when he hunts. There are too many people." She tugged the bag over to a large oak tree. "All his knights and guests, and if he sees me, he'll know. They say his knights can smell out witches."

"That's just not true, Mary. It's complete rubbish."

The horn sounded again, and Mary groaned. "He's going to stop and ask me questions. Be nice and friendly and then trap me in a witch net." Darting behind the tree, Mary pressed herself against it. "Hide, Della, or he'll take you, too."

Not knowing what else to do, Della followed. It was an ancient oak, wide enough to keep them both out of sight. Della could hear the yapping of hounds as the hunting party came closer. She could feel Mary quivering beside her, but when she glanced over, it was difficult to see her right away. Reaching out a hand, Della felt the scratchiness of Mary's dress, but it had changed to a woody, gray-brown color. So had her skin and hair. They even had the rough look of bark. Like a chameleon, Mary blended in perfectly with her surroundings.

As the thundering came closer, Della tried not to

breathe. Or move. She caught a flash of red jacket through the trees and hoped that Mary wouldn't start floating or sending bright green distress bubbles into the air. If they were discovered now, with Mary looking like an oak tree, they would both be hauled off to a dungeon. This was what real fear felt like, and Della screwed up her eyes as the hunt came galloping past. For a brief moment she almost cried out, feeling one of the hounds sniff at her legs. She didn't twitch a muscle until the animal, clearly not smelling a fox or deer or whatever it was they were hunting, dashed off.

Neither of the girls moved, waiting for the sound of hooves to be absorbed into the forest. Rough bark pressed against Della's cheek, but it wasn't until she heard birds chirping that she let out her breath with a whoosh. She was about to peel herself away from the oak when a strong hand grabbed her by the arm and did it for her.

Della screamed at the same moment as Mary, who was also being tugged backward.

"You blend in very nicely, my dear," the person holding them said, and Della looked up into a face as wrinkled and worn as a forgotten apple. It belonged to a woman who had a black shawl wrapped around her shoulders and wiry gray hair hanging loose. She was extremely old and extremely strong, her grip tight as an iron cuff.

Della gave a low moan of terror, trying to free herself, but her legs buckled beneath her. Just when she needed all her strength to fight and get away, she thought she might collapse from the shock.

"Please don't tell. Don't turn us in," Mary begged, which made Della worry that perhaps they offered big reward money for witches.

"Come with me," the woman said, and Della pushed against her with her free arm, as hard as she could.

"No, please, let us go," Della begged.

"I'm afraid I can't do that. You're witches."

"No, we're not," Della insisted, while Mary started to cry.

The woman gave a cackle of laughter. "Yes you are, and it's nothing to be ashamed of." Her voice was soft but serious. "Now stop fighting me. I'm not going to hurt you, but we can't talk out here. Woods have ears, and you never know who may be listening."

"Where are we going?" Della asked, not feeling quite so afraid.

"To my cottage." The old woman smiled, showing gaps between her teeth. "You'll be safe there."

Chapter Eight

....

A Cottage in the Woods

CLEARLY MARY HAD FORGOTTEN TO CENTER HER magic, because she still resembled an oak tree as the old woman marched them along. When Della tried to ask her how far they were going, the woman made a hushing noise, repeating, "Woods have ears, remember."

Luckily, they hadn't walked for more than a few minutes before they came upon a tiny cottage, tucked away in a clearing. There was a fence surrounding the property made of long, slender saplings woven between upright posts. In the middle of the fence was a wooden gate, and perched on each of the gateposts sat a huge (far bigger than Della had ever seen) eagle.

One of them stared right at her as the girls walked up. The other fixed its gaze on Mary. "That's Tambor and Bralin," the old woman said. "Tambor has the yellow tip on his wing. They keep an eye on things for me."

"I can see that," Della murmured, noticing the size and sharpness of their claws.

"You mustn't be scared. They won't hurt you," the old woman said, although Mary was clearly terrified, because she had started to turn translucent, as if trying to blend into thin air.

The old woman pushed open the gate and led the girls inside. "Careful where you step now. Don't go trampling on my plants." Della recognized bean and onion plants, but there were a great many unusual shrubs she had never seen before.

"I didn't know anyone lived in these woods," Mary said, looking all misty and out of focus.

"Lived here most of my life. You stay out of the way long enough and people forget about you. Those that know me call me Dame Bessie. And you're from Potts Bottom, I believe?"

"Mary Dutton of Potts Bottom."

Dame Bessie turned toward Della. "I don't remember seeing you here about."

"I'm Della Dupree," Della said, studying the old woman carefully to see if the name seemed familiar to her, but she didn't show any sign of recognition.

"And where do you hail from, Della Dupree?"

"Oh, a long way from here," Della said, thinking this was the understatement of the century. Wanting to change the conversation, Della asked, "Why do you need to stay out of the way?"

Dame Bessie opened the cottage door and paused a moment. She looked down at the girls. "Because I'm a witch too."

"You are?" Della burst out, relieved not to feel so alone in this strange place. "Thank goodness!"

Dame Bessie gave her a sharp look. "And people don't feel too fondly toward witches."

"No, I gathered that," Della said.

"Are you really a witch?" Mary whispered, halting on the doorstep and grabbing Della's hand.

"Got the magic when I was five," Dame Bessie said. "Can't ignore it. Can't squash it down and pretend it's not there. But I don't go around putting hexes on people."

"See, Mary," Della whispered with a grin. "I told you."

"So you truly don't think witches are evil?" Mary questioned Dame Bessie.

"Misunderstood but not evil. Do you?"

Mary thought for a moment and shook her head. "Everyone says they are, but I don't think so. And Della knows witches are good."

"Magic is a little different where I come from," Della confessed.

"They like witches there," Mary said.

"Is that so?" Dame Bessie gave Della a curious look, ushering the girls inside. "So what exactly are you doing in Potts Bottom, Della?"

Trying to stick to at least some of the facts, Della said, "Looking for someone. I got separated from the people I came with, and I'm actually trying to get home."

"But Tom Foolery stole her necklace and it's very precious and she can't leave without it."

"Well, that doesn't surprise me," Dame Bessie said. "That jester is a magpie. He can't resist glittery things."

The inside of the cottage was small and cozy. Dame Bessie picked up a smooth stick and waved it at her fireplace. The cool ashes burst into flames, and an iron kettle floated across the room, hanging itself on the hook above the fire.

"You have a wand?" Della said in surprise.

"Certain woods are excellent for conducting magic. This is beech," Dame Bessie said. "Now, I thought you might like some ginger tea? It's good for settling nerves."

"That's what my ma makes when I have an upset stomach," Mary said, and Della was relieved to see that she was back to her normal color.

Looking around the room, Della noticed a spinning wheel in the corner, spinning away on its own, making soft clicking noises as it worked.

"Who taught you how to do these things?" Della asked, feeling like she must be getting closer to Witch Dupree. This was magic being used as it was supposed to be, in a positive, helpful way.

Walking over to a table, Dame Bessie picked up a large cloth-bound book, the outside decorated in colorful vines, flowers, and winged beasts. "I was given this grimoire by my grandmother right before she died."

"Grimoire?" Mary said, looking puzzled.

"It's a book of magic, and this one was written many centuries ago by the first high priestess of magic."

"That's it? The actual one? Oh my gosh! It's in the—" Della was about to say "Royal Museum of Magic" but stopped herself in time. "I mean, I've heard about this book."

"It was written at a time when witches were allowed to practice freely, were encouraged to do what they loved."

"But why did it change?" Mary asked, moving closer to Della. "Why are people so scared of magic now?"

"Well, it's complicated, child. People felt threatened. And mostly because of one very bad witch who ruined it for the rest of us."

"Was that Raven Hunter?" Della said, remembering her from history class.

Dame Bessie gave Della a shrewd look. "Indeed it was. She fell in love with the king of England, but sadly he didn't feel the same way about her, so she changed him into a mouse. Put an invisibility spell on her castle so no one could ever find them and kept him as a pet." Della always giggled at this part, but her smile slipped away since Dame Bessie looked so sad. It wasn't just a story in a history book for her, and the old woman gave a heavy sigh. "That was the beginning of the end for witches. People began to hate for the sake of hating."

"But most witches aren't like that," Della said, putting an arm around Mary.

"You're right. They're not. But people are scared of what they don't understand. Magic frightens them because it can be powerful. Or because they would like to have our powers but don't. So they treat us badly. Try to lock us away. And that makes a number of witches very angry." Dame Bessie paused a moment, then said, "Which is the reason we have such an awful reputation." She waved her wand again and pointed it at a mouse that was scuttling across the floor. "Back outside, please. You can come in when the weather gets cold." The mouse lifted into the air and floated out of the window, where it was deposited gently on the grass.

"Can you take my magic away?" Mary asked.

Della nudged her gently. "Don't say that."

"I don't want it. It just makes me change color, and all these peculiar things happen."

"Which is why you have to learn to control it," Dame Bessie said soberly. "Otherwise you're going to get caught. Like poor Gwyneth over there." She nodded to the corner of the room, and Della realized that there was a tiny child tucked up under the heap of blankets, a tangle of messy curls spilling out.

"Oh my goodness," Della whispered, walking toward her. She peered down at the sleeping girl who couldn't have been much older than Robbie. She looked so small and vulnerable, and Della wondered how her family must be feeling. She couldn't bear it if something this awful happened to Lion. "Thank goodness you found her, Dame Bessie."

"She was playing in the cow barn when her magic started," Dame Bessie said. "Dipped her finger into the milk bucket and turned the milk blue. The poor thing got so scared, she ran and hid in the pigpen. But her magic was powerful, like new magic often is, and the pig she lay on top of started to fly." Dame Bessie shook her head sadly. "Caused quite a commotion, and now she can never go home again."

"She must be so frightened," Della said softly. "And homesick."

"That's the evil witch from Little Shamlington?" Mary whispered.

"Indeed it is. Terrifying, isn't she?" Dame Bessie pointed her wand at the kettle, and it lifted off the fire and floated over to the table, where three wooden mugs were waiting to be filled. In a somber voice she said, "You must learn how to survive without getting caught. And from what I've seen, neither of you have those skills. Hiding behind trees," Dame Bessie muttered, handing each girl a mug of ginger tea. Della felt as if she'd just been given a D for survival. "So come back tonight at the darkest hour, and I will show you what you need to stay safe."

"I'm scared of the dark," Mary said. "And how will I know when it's time? Or how to find my way here?"

"Trust me, you will. I'll send Tambor and Bralin to guide you."

"I don't think I'll be here," Della said hopefully. "Once I get my necklace back, I'm leaving right away."

"Well, Tambor will know. If you're here, he'll find you. If you have gone, then I wish you a speedy trip back."

"Is it mean of me to want you to stay?" Mary said, clutching Della's skirt.

"Oh, Mary, you have Dame Bessie to look after you now," Della said, hating to leave Mary but knowing she had no choice. "You'll be just fine."

"But not a word about this to anyone," Dame Bessie cautioned. "If we're found out, we will all be locked away."

"Where do they lock witches up?" Della asked, sipping her ginger tea.

"In the castle, child," Dame Bessie said gravely.

"The one you're going to," Mary added. "So please be careful, Della.

Chapter Nine

....

Castle Hepworth

DELLA HELPED MARY CARRY THE BAG OF KINDLING back as far as the edge of the village. Just as the huts came into view, a bird with an enormous beak, fluffy tail, and turkey-size body waddled out in front of them. "Oh, it's adorable," Della gushed as the bird ran into a tree. "And so clumsy and cute! I wish I could take it home with me."

"Stupid bird," Mary said. "They're always doing that."

"Wait, is that . . ." Della stared at the creature. "Is that a dodo?" she whispered in excitement, not wanting to frighten the bird away, although it hardly seemed aware that they were watching.

"We just call them stupid, because they run in front of carts and into trees. I've seen one leap right off the side of a hill. And they can't even fly."

"Must be a relation of the dodo," Della murmured, remembering that the dodo bird used to live in Mauritius and not Potts Bottom.

"I don't know." Mary shrugged. "I just know they get in the way."

Della wished she had a camera to take a picture of the bird. But she didn't, so she'd just have to memorize what it looked like. "We don't have these kinds of creatures where I come from," she said, staring at the peculiar-looking bird until it wandered away. "Well, that was exciting!"

"I can show you our chickens if you want to stay longer," Mary suggested. "They are much more interesting than that stupid bird."

"I can't stay longer, Mary. I'm sorry." Della hugged her good-bye. "It's going to be okay, though, you'll see." Mary didn't look so sure about this, and Della (who didn't feel too sure either) hugged her again before setting off toward the castle.

There was a rough path rutted with hoof marks, and the closer Della got, the more nervous she became. Halfway up the track a cart rumbled past, loaded with hay.

"Out of the way, girl," the driver yelled, scowling at Della. She stumbled onto the grass and stopped for a moment, staring up at the castle. Its stone walls and tiny narrow windows gave it an extremely unwelcoming air. So unwelcoming that Della decided to rest for a minute before going on. From somewhere close by she could hear the sound of running water, and following the gurgling, Della came upon a stream nestled in a wooded hollow. Kneeling beside it, she splashed water on her face, and since her braids were unraveling, tried to smooth them down, hoping to smarten herself up. But the result was more "damp mess" than "fair maiden," which didn't help Della's confidence much.

Two young deer trotted out of the woods to watch what she was doing.

"Hello," Della murmured, sitting quite still and holding out her hand. After a few moments the deer walked over and nestled against her, sniffing at her palm. "Hey, that tickles!"

Somebody laughed, and looking up, Della noticed a boy beside the riverbank, sitting against a tree. It was difficult to judge his age because his clothes were so old-fashioned, but Della guessed him to be around thirteen or fourteen. He was whittling a piece of wood with a knife, and catching her eye, the boy grinned. "You certainly have a way with animals."

"We understand each other," Della said with a smile, deciding he seemed friendly enough.

"Where are you heading?"

"To the castle. I'm looking for a job, although I'm a bit nervous about going up there. Lord Hepworth sounds a touch scary."

The boy laughed. "That's an odd way to phrase it, but yes, he can be."

"Do you know him?" Della stroked one of the deer on its muzzle.

"We're acquainted. We don't always see eye to eye, the lord and me. But you don't need to worry," he added. "You won't have much to do with him. It's Lady Hepworth who's in charge of the household."

"What are you carving?" Della asked, walking over, the two little deer trotting along behind.

The boy held up a smooth wooden crescent. "It's a new moon, see."

"Oh, that's beautiful," Della said. "You're very talented."

"Here, you can have it if you like. It's made from beech wood. My father doesn't like it when I carve, so I try not to do it at home."

"Are you sure?"

"I have to go anyway." The boy scrambled to his feet and presented the moon to Della. She took it without hesitating, and a tingling rushed through her fingers, as if the wood had somehow triggered her magic. Inhaling sharply, Della slipped the carving into her pocket, not wanting to attract attention.

"Thank you."

"You're most welcome." The boy gave a deep bow, and before she could ask him his name, he took off at a run.

Della waited a few minutes before pulling out the carving to examine. It was smooth and fine grained, the wood a pale silvery blond with a tiny acorn etched on one side. The second her fingers touched the surface she felt her magic stirring again. A powerful sensation that reminded her of the danger she was in. Not that she needed reminding, and gathering up her courage, Della headed back toward the path.

It was strange to see a castle on top of Clackton Ridge, and Della had to stop halfway across the drawbridge, holding on to the side because she felt suddenly dizzy, like it was all too much to take in. There was actual water in the moat, and off to the left she could see a group of knights practicing jousting. They were galloping about on horses, trying to knock each other off with long poles. In fact it all looked rather similar to the medieval fair Potts Bottom held every summer. The only thing missing was the smell of frying donuts.

Two ladies strolled past, dressed in embroidered silk gowns, with ribbons and flowers braided into their hair. They glanced briefly at Della and then (as if she wasn't worth noticing) away again, taking with them her last shred of confidence.

For the longest time Della didn't move. She stood frozen on the drawbridge as if waiting for something to happen, someone to help her, but no one stopped to ask if she was all right, and Della shut her eyes for a moment, terrified of being so alone.

"I really don't think I can do this," she whispered, but she had no choice if she wanted to find the travel amulet. Before losing her nerve completely, Della took a deep breath and forced herself to finish walking into the courtyard and up to the huge wooden door. She banged the heavy iron knocker against it, and the door opened almost at once, taking her a little off guard.

"And who are you?" a man dressed in tights and a tunic inquired, looking at Della as if she were a bad smell.

Clearing her throat and hoping she didn't look too young, Della said, "I'm looking for work. I wondered if you might have any?" She paused and added, "I—I know Tom Foolery."

The man rolled his eyes. "Everyone knows Tom Foolery. He's not here. Won't be back until the morrow. What kind of work can you do?"

"Anything."

"Really." The man folded his arms and studied her. "Mrs. Chambers is always on the hunt for good, strong girls, but you don't look like you're used to hard work."

"Oh, I am," Della said, nodding. "I clean, and make beds, and can help in the kitchen." Although she wasn't sure her mother would agree with this.

"Is that so?"

Della waited for him to ask her age, but clearly that wasn't important. Nor where she had come from or if her parents knew. In fact the only thing he seemed to care about was if she could lift two pails of water at once.

"I'm much stronger than I look," Della said.

"We'll let Mrs. Chambers be the judge of that. She runs the household for her ladyship. Come along." And the man led Della across an enormous hall that had a long table stretching down it, and a smaller table on a raised platform at one end. There was a fireplace so big Della could have walked inside it, and thick tapestries hanging on the walls. The room was dark and, like all the homes she had been in so far, smelled rather strongly of smoke. A rat scuttled past her, and Della gave a soft cry.

"Better get used to those." The man grinned. "We've got plenty."

They walked down a hallway that led to an entirely

separate building, past a laundry room crowded with women leaning over tubs, scrubbing clothes. It was loud and steamy, but the kitchen was worse, filled with the clatter of pots and sweaty bodies. There was a whole pig lying on the table and a pile of dead blackbirds waiting to be plucked. Averting her gaze, Della decided that the second she got home she was becoming a vegetarian. One woman rolled out pastry for a pie, and a huge cauldron bubbled away over an open hearth. There were young girls chopping and sweeping and boys bringing in armfuls of wood. The noise level was deafening, and Mrs. Chambers turned out to be the beefy red-faced woman yelling out orders. She looked Della up and down, prodded her arm, and said, "You'll go where you're needed, girl. Penny a day and you start now."

"Thank you," Della said as a pot clattered to the floor.

"Speak up. I can't hear you."

"I said thank you," Della shouted, reminding herself that this was only for one day. It had to be, she thought, trying not to cry. She couldn't stay here for longer than that. She just couldn't.

For the next four hours Della chopped up a mountain of cabbage and onions for a stew, scrubbed out pots, and carried in pail after pail of water from an outdoor well. Her arms ached, and the skin on her hands cracked, and every time she slopped water on the floor (which happened most trips), she got yelled at. Worst of all, Della sighted at least six more rats, hauling off bits of cheese and vegetable peelings. There was a continuous chatter of gossip, and a great deal of the conversations seemed to be about the witch from Little Shamlington.

"I saw her fly over the castle," one of the girls sweeping the floor said. "She looked terrifying. You could see the evil in her eyes. Cackling away, she was, and I swear she threw a spell right at me."

"No she didn't," Della whispered, thinking of little Gwyneth curled up in the corner of Dame Bessie's hut. The poor thing was probably terrified, experiencing her magic for the first time.

"Don't stand there dawdling," Mrs. Chambers called out, poking Della gently in the back with a wooden spoon. "There's more water to be brought in."

"And if you meet that witch out there, throw a pail of water over her quick," a young boy said. "My granny says she'll melt right away." Della stared at him in amazement, stunned that they actually believed such things. "You have to protect yourself from the witches," he added. Although as far as Della could see, it was the witches who were in need of protection.

Chapter Ten

....

A Midnight Flight and a New Wand

AFTER LORD AND LADY HEPWORTH AND THEIR GUESTS had eaten, Della and the rest of the servants were offered some leftover blackbird pie (which Della refused), a selection of heavily salted mystery meats (also refused), and some strange beans dripping in honey and spices (which she wished she had refused). It was not a meal Della wanted to repeat, and she felt a fresh pang of sadness at the loss of her wand. A plate of lasagna or a warm apple pie spell would have made everything seem a whole lot more bearable right about now.

Della had been working so hard she didn't notice

that the light had faded until Mrs. Chambers handed her a rush mat and bid her good night. Evidently there was no such thing as a bedroom, and Della watched in dismay as the servants laid their mats down wherever there was a space. There didn't seem to be any privacy at all, or proper washing facilities for that matter (as far as Della could tell), which gave the air a rather powerful tang. She did manage to scrub her teeth with a carrot, but her scalp itched and her skin felt all sticky, and she would have given anything for a really hot shower.

Most of the warm places near the fire had been taken, so Della spread her mat out by the kitchen door. She could feel a draft blowing in, but at least it was easier to breathe over here. Even though she was exhausted, Della lay awake for a while, listening to a symphony of snoring, and suffering from so much homesickness she could barely swallow around the lump in her throat. Girls like Mary and the tiny witch from Little Shamlington were definitely going to need some of Dame Bessie's survival skills if they didn't want to get caught. In fact, if she stayed here much longer, she would too, especially without her wand. But getting to Dame Bessie's seemed an absolute impossibility. There was no way she was going to go traipsing around the woods in the dark, and with that thought swirling in her head, Della finally drifted off to sleep, only to be woken a short while later by the low cry of a bird and a soft peck-pecking against the door.

Remembering that Dame Bessie had promised to send Tambor, Della got up and, as quietly as she could, opened the door. There, sitting right outside as if he'd been waiting for her, was the eagle. It was definitely Tambor, because she could just make out the yellow tip on his wing. And the sight of the eagle was surprisingly comforting. "Do you want me to follow you?" Della whispered, but Tambor didn't move. He looked up at her and spread his enormous wings, which were wider than a full-grown man's outstretched arms. After a few moments he gestured with his head, and Della understood that he wanted her to climb on.

"I'm really okay to walk," she whispered, but Tambor gave what was clearly an irritated huff. Feeling a little worried he might decide to pick her up with his claws if she didn't obey, Della very gingerly crawled on top of the bird, lying almost flat on her belly and wrapping her arms around his neck. Almost immediately she felt the muscles in Tambor's back ripple as he launched himself into the air. Della gasped and then laughed as they gained height, swooping straight up. "No flying above the treetops," she cried, which was the rule for all year four girls. Not paying any attention, Tambor flew higher, much higher than Della had ever been. She clung on tight as they soared across the meadows that bordered Potts Bottom and toward the shadowy expanse of woods. Della pressed her cheek against the warm feathered neck of the bird. He carried her as if she weighed no more than a handful of extra feathers, and when they began to descend, Della clung on harder, worried that she might slip right off. She could see the outline of Dame Bessie's cottage below them, and the second they landed, the door was flung open.

"Thank you, Tambor. That was amazing," Della whispered, stroking the bird on the head. Her hands ached from holding on so tight, and her legs felt a little shaky as she slid off.

"Quickly now," Dame Bessie called from the doorway. "Don't dawdle."

Della hurried toward the cottage, and as soon as she had stepped inside, Dame Bessie slammed the door shut. "Follow me, please." She pointed her stick at the fireplace, and the hearthstone slid open, exposing a steep flight of stairs. "Careful where you tread."

"Is Mary here?" Della asked, following behind. The dark narrow staircase spiraled round and round, eventually opening up into a room full of flickering candles. And there, sitting on colorful rugs spread across the floor, were Mary, Gwyneth, and three other girls.

"Della!" Mary squealed, leaping up to give her a hug. "I've been showing Dame Bessie how you helped me stop changing color," she said, showing off her breathing.

"That's excellent, Mary. Well done!" And taking Mary by the hand, Della settled them both on the rug.

"This is Della Dupree," Dame Bessie said. "She will be joining us."

"Just until I go home. Which will hopefully be tomorrow," Della added softly.

"That may be, but as long as you are here, you need to learn to survive." Dame Bessie gestured at the group. "All these girls come from neighboring villages. You know Mary and Gwyneth already, of course, and this is Willow"—she pointed at a girl with dark, water-straight hair—"and that's Faye with the braids, and over there with the cat on her knee and the mess of curls is Isolda. They are witches just like you."

"Yes, we're all so evil," Faye said, making a menacing face. The other girls laughed, but not Dame Bessie.

"This is something we don't joke about, Faye. It's remarks like that which give witchcraft a bad name."

"Sorry," Faye apologized, looking down.

"You are here to learn how to protect yourselves," Dame Bessie said. "To keep your magic locked away and out of sight. But sometimes it will leak out," she added soberly. "And you may find yourselves in grave danger. . . ."

Gwyneth started to cry. "I don't want to be a witch."

"None of us do," Faye muttered.

"That's why we have to listen to Dame Bessie, Gwyneth," Willow said. "She can help us stay safe."

"Don't worry," Della whispered, patting her lap. "You can sit here if you like." And after hesitating a moment, Gwyneth climbed onto Della's knee, settling against her just like Lion always did.

"So today we will practice shape-shifting," Dame Bessie continued, "turning ourselves into animals for a quick and easy escape."

"No, we can't!" Della burst out, looking around to see if anyone else was as shocked as she was. More softly, so as not to scare Gwyneth, she said, "That's illegal. That's so illegal." Ms. Cray would have had a stroke if she'd heard this.

"It may be illegal, but if it saves you from being thrown in the dungeons, then you have no other choice."

"What about the witches' code of honor?" Della said, something all Ruthersfield girls had drummed into them from the first day of school. "Where I come from, we're supposed to use our magic for the good, to help people. And never, under any circumstances, to practice shape-shifting." Judging from the girls' puzzled expressions, Della realized none of them had heard of the witches' code of honor, and she couldn't help thinking Witch Dupree was going to have her work cut out when she finally showed up. Because right now it was impossible to imagine there would ever be a Ruthersfield Academy.

"There's a knights' code of honor," Willow said. "My brother has to learn it because he's in training with Lord Hepworth. Be chivalrous, be brave, face down all dragons, and rescue any and all damsels in distress."

"Well, the only code of honor you need to worry about is keeping yourselves safe," Dame Bessie said. "Now take out your wands, girls, and let's begin."

"We get wands?" Della asked in excitement.

"To make lasagna!" Mary whispered, licking her lips.

Willow held up a smooth, slender stick. "Mine is apple wood."

"And mine is hawthorn," Faye said. "My spells are much stronger when I use hawthorn. I can turn into a really tiny animal and suck all the water out of a river if I need to cross it quickly."

"Woods have different properties," Dame Bessie explained, carrying a basket of sticks over to Della and Mary. "Some work better than others, depending on the time of your birth."

"I'm a snow baby," Isolda told them. "Born in a blizzard, so my wood is oak."

"So is Gwyneth's," Dame Bessie said, handing the little girl a wand.

"Isn't she a bit young?" Della worried as Gwyneth got up and started to dance about, waving the stick.

"No. All witches must learn to protect themselves," Dame Bessie replied sharply. "And when were you born?" she asked Mary.

"During lambing," Mary said.

"Cherry might work well," Dame Bessie mused, offering Mary a stick. The second Mary held it, a stream of violets puffed out of the end. "Oh, far too strong. Try pear," Dame Bessie said, exchanging the stick for another. This time the tip glowed a soft purple, and she gave a satisfied nod. "Much better. Now, how about you?"

"June twenty-first," Della said. "Midsummer Eve, the shortest night of the year."

"Ahh." Dame Bessie nodded, as if this made perfect sense. "Since you are a child of the solstice then, I think you should try this." She plucked up a smooth, silvery-colored stick stripped of its bark and handed it to Della. "Beech is an ancient wood. I have a feeling this will be a good fit." And as soon as Della touched it, her fingers started to tingle in the same way they had when she'd held the little carved moon the boy had given her. This was not like a Ruthersfield wand, the one all the girls got, blended with different types of wood, weighted down with unicorn horn to keep their spells grounded and contained, and highly polished to protect it from scratches. This felt more like a lightning rod, as if there was nothing between Della and her magic, and she sensed she would have to be extremely careful when she used it.

"Now think of the animal you would like to change into. Something fast is good, that can get away quickly. A deer, or a hare, and field mice are excellent, because they can disappear easily. So are spiders and beetles, but you want to avoid being stepped on."

"I'll be a field mouse," Faye said.

"What about a swallow?" Willow asked. "So we could fly."

"Or a snail," Mary suggested. "I could hide in my shell."

"A wabbit." Gwyneth giggled. "I love wabbits."

"I'm going to be a cat," Isolda said, stroking the animal in her lap. "Like Tiger Balm."

"Go with what feels right to you," Dame Bessie said. "When the first high priestess of magic wrote down the spell, she often changed into a griffin, but that is far too obvious for our purposes. We need to blend in, not stand out."

"A hare," Della murmured, trying not to think of how much trouble she'd be in if anyone knew what she was doing. Well, "trouble" was an understatement. She'd be locked up in Scrubs, the high-security prison just for witches, for the rest of her life.

"Now tap your stick against your leg and whisper 'mutatiarno' very softly, so as not to draw attention to yourself." Dame Bessie demonstrated, turning into a mouse. The girls watched her scuttle across the floor. There was a smell of burning toffee, and then Dame Bessie appeared again.

"How do you change back without your wand?" Della asked nervously.

"The reversal spell is woven right into the magic, so you just have to chant 'mutatiarno' again to release it. Of course, you may not be able to go back for your wand," Dame Bessie added somberly. "But at least you will be safe." She gestured at the girls. "Now you try."

One by one, Della watched them turn into a field mouse, a cat, a snail, and a baby rabbit. Willow flew around the room as a swallow.

"What are you waiting for, Della?" Dame Bessie inquired.

"I'm not sure I can. It feels so wrong."

"If someone finds out you're a witch and sends an

army of knights after you brandishing swords, are you just going to stand there?"

"Mutatiarno," Della said, tapping the beech stick against her thigh. Immediately she felt a powerful surge of energy rush through her body. This was probably what getting an electric shock felt like. The blood in her head pulsed, and her arms and legs tingled as if she were being squeezed out of her body. Then the next thing Della knew, she was hopping across the room, leaping about on a set of strong back legs. It was a deeply unsettling feeling, being yourself but not yourself, performing this sort of raw, ancient magic that could transform you into something else. There was a part of Della that wanted to hop outside, to smell the grass and feel the wind and see what it was like to race across the fields. And she suddenly understood why this kind of magic had been banned. It was intoxicating and addictive and (considering she almost stepped on Mary's snail shell when she turned back) extremely dangerous.

....

Chapter Eleven

Della Meets Lord Hepworth

DAME BESSIE LED THE GIRLS BACK UPSTAIRS AND threw another log on the fire. "We meet again in five nights' time, when I'll show you how to wipe clean a memory. So if anyone discovers you're a witch, you can take that knowledge right out of their heads. Help them forget."

"But that's mind magic," Della whispered to Faye. Messing about with someone's thoughts was just as much a crime as shape-shifting. "We cannot be learning how to do that."

"If you have something to say, Della, there's no need to whisper," Dame Bessie remarked, leading Gwyneth over to her pallet in the corner. "Besides, I can hear you quite clearly." She tucked a blanket around the little girl. "This is strong, dangerous magic, and should, of course, not be used unless absolutely necessary."

"I think I'm going to need such a spell," Faye sighed. "My mother already suspects. I used magic to start the fire two days ago because the wood was so damp, and I know she had a suspicion."

"But she wouldn't say anything, would she?" Della said. "I mean, she's your mother."

Faye didn't answer, although the look on her face told Della all she needed to know. Della tried to imagine what it would be like, having your own parents turn against you. But she couldn't. A pang of longing hit her in the gut, and she shut her eyes for a moment, thinking about how much she missed her family.

Dame Bessie clapped her hands for attention. "We're about to go outside, girls, so hoods over your heads and no noise. Take your branch from behind the woodpile and leave as quietly as you can."

"Why do we need a branch?" Mary said, slipping her hand into Della's.

"To fly home on," Faye told them. "Mine is hawthorn, because that's my special wood."

"I didn't even know witches had special woods until tonight," Della said, thinking how much witchcraft had changed. This strong bond between magic and nature had somehow been lost over time. Magic in the twenty-first century felt all polished and tidy and controlled. Wands in cellophane-wrapped boxes and broomsticks that were so highly varnished you couldn't even feel a connection to the wood. Not like the branch Dame Bessie handed her.

"It's beech, dear, like your wand. And yours is pear, Mary. Don't take the leaves off the back end, because they help with balance."

"But I don't know how to fly," Mary said.

"Don't worry—I'm sure we'll get a lesson," Della reassured her. At Ruthersfield the girls weren't even allowed near a broomstick until they had done two weeks of flying theory in the classroom.

"I'm afraid there will be no lessons," Dame Bessie said. "If I were caught offering instruction . . ." There was no need for Dame Bessie to finish this sentence, because by now Della had a pretty good idea what would happen.

"Just remember to fly as high as you can, and only at night," Willow told them, stepping one leg over her apple branch. "That way if anyone does see, we usually get mistaken for a bat."

"Are you serious?" Della said in a panic.

"And don't let go," Dame Bessie advised.

"I'm frightened," Mary whispered.

Della was about to tell her they could fly together, but Dame Bessie said, "I'll send Bralin with you, Mary. Follow him, and if you fall, he will catch you." She looked at Della. "You, I imagine, have some experience?"

"A bit," Della admitted, thinking that a tree branch was very different from her training broom with cruise control and an altitude beeper that stopped you from going too high. And, she quickly found out, not only more uncomfortable but much harder to control.

"Remember, five nights hence at the witching hour," Dame Bessie said as Della took off with a sharp jerk. She gave a muffled scream as the branch juddered and shook, climbing into the air. Trying to remain calm, Della flew past the treetops, gripping the branch so tight she could feel rough bark pressing into her palms. The cold stung her cheeks, and she was terrified to go any higher, but at least dawn hadn't broken yet, so there was still enough darkness to offer protection.

When she finally saw Clackton Ridge looming up ahead, and the great gray outline of the castle, Della heaved a sigh of relief. Keeping her height, she decided to land behind the stables, in case there were knights on watch. Not that they'd be looking upward, expecting an attack from the air, but she didn't want to take any chances. Della swooped down far faster than she was used to, biting her lip to stop herself from screaming again, which she very much wanted to do. Trying to keep control of the branch, she aimed at a pile of hay. It wasn't the smoothest of landings, but at least the hay was soft, and she rolled right off, lying still for a moment while her head stopped spinning. Getting up slowly, Della decided to leave the branch behind the stables. She didn't want to bring it closer to the castle in case somebody chopped it up for firewood, which, from the way her luck had been going so far, seemed very likely to happen. Suddenly feeling exhausted, Della leaned against the stable wall, tiredness and worry flooding through her. What if she never got out of this place? Her legs started to shake, and she pressed her hands against her stomach, giving a frightened whimper. But she couldn't think like that. She had to believe everything was going to be okay and by Wednesday, in five nights' time, she'd be safely back home again.

Slipping inside, Della lay down on her mat, managing a short burst of sleep before being woken right up again. Cold morning air blew on her face as the kitchen stirred to life. Cooks were already chopping and mixing, and a pan of spicy stew bubbled away over the fire, covering up the stench of unwashed bodies with cinnamon and cloves.

A cart rumbled into the courtyard, dropping off a massive amount of bread, still warm from the baker's ovens. Della was put to work slicing the tops off each loaf.

"Make haste," Mrs. Chambers ordered. "His lordship and guests are going hunting again, so let's not keep them waiting." She hustled over and dipped a spoon in the stew, taking a taste and spitting it right back out. "Myrtle, did you make this swill?" she screamed. "It's disgusting. Not fit to feed the pigs."

A woman who had to be Myrtle blushed deep scarlet. "Sorry, mam, I dropped the bag of salt in."

"What's his lordship going to say when there's no pheasant in the pot? This is a catastrophe. You can pack your bags and head right back to Deckle Mead."

Myrtle started to sob, and there was so much commotion going on that no one noticed Della dart over to the fireplace and wave her beech stick over the pot, pretending to use it to take a taste. She murmured a quick transformation spell, which the girls often performed at school lunch to change extremely dry meatloaf into fabulously juicy steak.

"And what on earth are you doing?" Mrs. Chambers screeched as the pot belched out a cloud of orange smoke, turning the nasty-tasting pheasant into a delicious chicken curry. "What went in there?"

Della froze, suddenly realizing what she had done.

This wasn't a potions class at Ruthersfield. And it wasn't the twenty-first century. She'd used magic in Castle Hepworth, which wasn't just stupid, but unbelievably dangerous.

"I was trying to help," Della said, tossing in a carrot to look as if she knew what she was doing. "My mum—I mean my mother—taught me how to save a heavily salted stew."

"Ummph." Mrs. Chambers trotted over to the pot. She took a tiny sip and then another and another, each spoonful getting bigger. "This will do nicely, Della." She gave a brisk nod. "As for you, Myrtle, one more mistake and it will be back to Deckle Mead, I can promise you that."

"Oh, thank you, Mrs. Chambers," Myrtle said, throwing Della a grateful look.

"Right, then. Let's see what his lord and ladyship think." And, unhooking the pot of pheasant stew (which was actually chicken curry), Mrs. Chambers led a procession of maids hefting platters of cold meats, jugs of ale, and a great many baskets of bread down the corridor to the great hall. It wasn't long before she returned, beckoning for Della to follow her. "Lord Hepworth wants to see you."

"He does?" Della said, worried they could taste the magic. "Why?"

"The stew, of course. Now come along."

"Do I have to?" Della said, but Mrs. Chambers was already marching off, and Della hurried after her, trying to remember how to turn herself into a hare in case she needed a quick getaway.

The tables in the great hall were crowded with people drinking ale and eating off the crusts of bread Della had cut, which appeared to take the place of plates. In the middle of the shorter, raised table sat a bearded man in a wine-colored robe with a green tunic underneath, who Della guessed (correctly) had to be Lord Hepworth. A well-padded woman wearing a purple satin gown and an elaborate beaded headpiece sat on one side of him, and on his other, much to Della's surprise, was the boy she had met by the river, the one who had given her the carved moon. Although judging from his place at the table, Della suspected he was more than an acquaintance of Lord Hepworth's.

"This is Della Dupree," Mrs. Chambers announced, and Della could feel herself blushing as everyone turned to stare.

"You made this?" Lord Hepworth gestured at his wooden bowl. His face was red and a little puffy, and Della couldn't tell if he was angry or overexcited. She nodded, gripping the beech wand in her pocket.

"It's excellent." He smiled. "I've never had pheasant taste so good. Not too salty at all."

The woman in the purple dress leaned over and kissed Lord Hepworth on his cheek. "My husband is a happy man."

Lord Hepworth patted the boy beside him. "Ivan, too. He's on his third helping. Gathering strength for his jousting match, eh!"

Della noticed the boy subtly roll his eyes, as if he wasn't too keen on the idea of jousting.

"You're new here, Mrs. Chambers tells me," Lady Hepworth inquired.

"I—I arrived yesterday," Della said, trying not to look at the floor.

"Give the girl an extra halfpenny, Mrs. Chambers," the lord shouted out. "You don't want to lose her."

There was a great deal of cheering from the guests at this, and Della wondered how much ale they had consumed. Far too much for eight o'clock in the morning, she decided.

"Very good, my lord," Mrs. Chambers said.

He dismissed them with a wave of his hand, holding up his cup for more ale.

"And tonight, my friends, you are in for a treat," Lord Hepworth bellowed down the table. "Tom Foolery will be here to amaze and delight."

"Tom Foolery." Della stopped and glanced back.

"He's the castle jester." Mrs. Chambers gave an indulgent giggle. "Cheers you up when you're full of the miseries."

And steals your only way home, Della thought. Forcing herself to smile, she said, "I can't wait to meet him."

Chapter Twelve

....

A Bold-Faced Lie

D ELLA SPENT THE REST OF THE DAY TAKING ORDERS
from Mrs. Chambers and trying to keep an eye
out for Tom Foolery. He had taken over from Gwyneth
(the witch from Little Shamlington) as the main topic
of conversation.

"He's so funny," one of the maids said.

"And clever," another replied. "Do you remember
when he made that apple roll down the table without
touching it and pulled a ribbon out of Master Ivan's
mouth?"

"I laugh every time I hear his bells coming," Mrs.
Chambers said.

The kitchen door opened, and one of the stable boys rushed in. "Lord Hepworth isn't too happy. Master Ivan just got knocked off his horse. Again."

"They're holding a big jousting tournament here next week," Mrs. Chambers explained. "And Master Ivan is entering. He's meant to bring honor on the Hepworth name, but judging from what I've seen so far, that is not going to happen."

"Good thing Tom Foolery is back tonight," Myrtle said, chopping up a turnip. "His lordship's going to need some cheering up."

"What time is he getting back?" Della asked.

"You'll know when you hear his bells," Mrs. Chambers replied, smiling.

It couldn't be soon enough, Della thought, feeling more and more desperate to get back home. She had discovered that the castle toilet consisted of a bench with a hole in the middle. Down below was the moat, and the smell from this chamber was so disgusting that Della had been forced to put a lavender-scented spell on the room; otherwise it was literally impossible to breathe in there. This was clearly a great improvement, because Lady Hepworth had actually come out smiling.

But Della couldn't perfume the entire castle, and when the stench in the kitchen got to be too much, she slipped outside for some fresh air, usually heading for the stables. This was her favorite place, because she could check to make sure her beech branch was still there, and the grassy, animal smells of hay and horses were a welcome relief after the castle.

On one of her trips Della was leaning over a stall door, stroking the muzzle of a reddish-brown horse, when she caught sight of Ivan, sitting on a hay bale in the corner. He was whittling away at a small piece of wood that looked to be in the shape of an animal, only this time he didn't seem so cheerful.

"Hello again," Della said, realizing she felt slightly annoyed with him. "You didn't tell me you were Lord Hepworth's son."

He glanced up at her. "I try not to think about it if I can help it."

"I would never have called him scary if I'd known."

Ivan kept on whittling. "Well, he can be scary."

"Sorry about your jousting match," Della said. "I hope you didn't hurt yourself."

"It wasn't a proper match. More of a lesson, and no, I didn't hurt myself. I think it pains my father more than me when I fall off." Ivan sighed rather deeply. "I hate jousting."

"Then why do you do it?" Della asked, kissing the velvety muzzle of the horse.

"Because I have to. Family honor. My father's hosting a tournament here, and I'm expected not to disgrace myself. There's no chance I'll win, but he's going to be so ashamed if I get knocked out in the first round. Which will happen," Ivan added with another deep sigh.

"Can't you tell him you don't want to enter? He seems much nicer than I was expecting. I'm sure he wouldn't mind."

"Oh, he would. You have no idea. The man can be terrifying."

"Sounds like Ms. Cray," Della murmured, thinking of her headmistress. She pointed at the carving in Ivan's hands. "Is that a horse?"

"It's Chestnut, my steed." Ivan held up a perfectly sculptured miniature horse.

"How do you do that?"

"I don't know." Ivan shrugged. "I'm just good with my hands. How do you make pheasant stew taste so good?"

For a moment Della wondered what would happen if she said "magic." Not that she would risk it. But Ivan seemed so nice and understanding, it was hard to believe he would have her locked up. "We both have our skills," Della said.

"Except according to my father, wood carving is

peasants' work. And not what a lord's son should be doing."

"And what does your mother say?"

"I don't think she minds as much, but she would never voice that opinion to my father."

"Oh." Della sounded surprised. "Well, good luck with the jousting." She gave Chestnut another kiss. "I'd better go. I don't want to get into trouble with Mrs. Chambers."

"Wait." Ivan stood up. "It's been nice talking to you. You seem"—he hesitated a moment—"different from other girls. And I don't mean that disrespectfully," he added.

Della laughed a little wistfully. "I feel different," she agreed. "You're not wrong there." A faint sound of bells drifted into the stables. "Hey, do you hear that?" Della cried. "Is it bells?"

"Sounds like Tom Foolery has returned."

"Oh goodness. I must go."

"Can we take a walk on the morrow?"

"I'm not sure your father would want you walking with a kitchen maid. And I don't even know if I'm going to be here, Ivan. I might have to go home at short notice."

"Is someone in your family sick?" Ivan asked, looking worried.

"Not sick, but there is a family crisis going on," Della said, which felt close enough to the truth. She gave Ivan a wave and, with her heart beating like a trapped bird, hurried out of the barn, anxious to find Tom Foolery.

Della followed the sound of bells, which led her straight back into the kitchen. And there was Tom Foolery, eating a piece of bread and honey, surrounded by a crowd of workers. He licked his sticky fingers and gave a deep bow in front of Mrs. Chambers. "That was delicious, madam." Straightening up with a jingle, Tom Foolery pulled a little bouquet of pansies out of Mrs. Chambers's ear. She slapped her chest and roared with laughter.

"Oh, you are too much, Tom. That is clever."

"And shouldn't this fish be cooking for the lord's supper?" Tom said, reaching into Myrtle's apron pocket and tugging out a trout by the tail.

"Oh my goodness," Myrtle gasped. "How did that get in there?"

"It is good to have you home," Mrs. Chambers chuckled. "I bet you cheered up his lordship's cousin."

Tom Foolery gave a proud smile. "When I pulled a rabbit from under his nightcap, he laughed so hard he almost fell out of bed!"

"I bet he did," Mrs. Chambers agreed.

"And now, if you'll excuse me, I must head to my chamber to rest before entertaining Lord Hepworth's guests."

Managing to catch the jester's gaze, Della saw a flash of recognition in his eyes. He quickly dropped to the ground and turned a series of somersaults across the room, clearly wanting to escape. Della rushed after him, her panic overriding the fear of confronting him.

"Tom Foolery, please wait," Della called out. "It's nice to see you again."

Turning around, the jester hesitated a moment, acting as if he had only just noticed her. "Ahh, it's the girl from the woods."

Della swallowed, relieved he at least acknowledged her. "You were so kind to my friend that day, cheering her up."

Tom Foolery made a sad face and mimicked tears streaming down his cheeks.

"Yes, she was very upset," Della agreed. "But you made her feel so much better."

"That's what I'm here for," Tom Foolery said, narrowing his eyes at Della. "What are you here for, I wonder?"

"Mrs. Chambers gave me a job. I—I'm working here now." Della could feel her heart throbbing, and her mouth had gone dry. "Do you think you might give me back my necklace?" she said. "I know you didn't mean to, but you forgot to return it. And . . . and . . . it's very special to me. I can't go home without it." Della could see Mrs. Chambers giving her a strange look. "I would get into a lot of trouble."

Tom Foolery cocked his head to one side. "A necklace, you say." He gave an elaborate shrug. "I don't remember."

"You must remember." Della could hear the wobble in her voice. "Please just give it back."

"Oh, but I would if I could," Tom Foolery said, turning his pockets inside out. "Empty, empty, as you can see." He waved his hands over them and then, reaching back inside, pulled out an onion from each one.

"Well, I never!" Mrs. Chambers shrieked in amazement. "How in the world? You are clever!"

The jester grinned and tossed the onions to Mrs. Chambers.

"Please," Della begged. "It couldn't have fallen off. I know you took it."

"He's not a thief. Now that's enough," Mrs. Chambers broke in, putting an end to the conversation.

Tom Foolery held Della's gaze steady for a few seconds, as if challenging her to disagree. He seemed about to say something, then just as quickly changed his mind and pranced out of the room. Della sank down on a stool. She covered her face with her hands, terrified to think about what any of this meant. That she might never see her family again, or her friends, or go to school, or stop in at Poppy's bakery for a cupcake . . . But she had to think about it, because the necklace was gone. And unless a miracle occurred, she was going to be stuck here, in the smelly, witch-hating thirteenth century for the rest of her life.

Chapter Thirteen

....

Della Explores

ENOUGH MOPING," MRS. CHAMBERS ADMONISHED. Della stood at the table beside her, attempting to pluck a chicken. "You look like the world is about to end."

"That's how I feel," Della said, thinking that pulling feathers out of a chicken was one of the worst jobs she had ever done.

"Oh now, stop this. I'm sure your family will understand about the necklace. If it was such a treasure, they shouldn't have let you wear it."

"They didn't. I took it without asking. You have no idea how much trouble I'm in, Mrs. Chambers."

"I dare say it's not as bad as you believe," Mrs.

Chambers said, tossing chicken parts into a bowl of sour milk.

"Yes it is. I can promise you." After a few more feeble plucks Della said, "You don't know anyone else called Della Dupree, do you, Mrs. Chambers? She's a sort of relative of mine. I was named after her, and I'm trying to find her."

"No, I can't say I do." Mrs. Chambers shook her head. "Is this Della going to get you out of trouble?"

"I'm hoping she might if I can ever track her down." Della sighed. "I thought she was supposed to live near here."

"Well, I'll ask around. There are folks from all over at the castle. Someone may know of her."

"Thank you, Mrs. Chambers. I really appreciate it."

The rest of the afternoon passed in a fog, with Della growing more and more anxious. The thought of being stuck here was so distressing that she stopped paying attention to the pile of carrots she was chopping and sliced her finger instead.

"Ouch!" Della winced as blood dripped onto the table.

"Stupid child," Mrs. Chambers barked. "Watch what you're doing."

"Wrap this around," Myrtle said, throwing Della a piece of dirty cloth. "It will stanch the bleeding."

"I—I have to clean it," Della cried, holding up her finger and rushing outside to the well. Except what was the point of cleaning it and then wrapping a dirty cloth around the wound? She would probably end up with blood poisoning anyway. Stumbling behind the stables so she wouldn't be seen, Della took out her beech wand and in a shaky voice whispered a healing spell, waving the stick over her cut. She still wasn't used to the powerful tingling that rushed up her arm whenever she used it. But the spell worked the way it was meant to, and Della watched in satisfaction as the wound on her finger closed up. She wiped the blood away and then tied the cloth around where the cut had been, not wanting to draw attention to the fact that her finger had miraculously healed.

By the time Della unrolled her rush mat, she had never felt so alone and unhappy in her life. She could hear the scratching of rats as they sniffed about the floor, helping themselves to scraps. Della tucked herself up in a tight ball, terrified that one of them would start nibbling her toes. Her throat grew tight, and she dug her nails into her palms, trying not to cry. Because once she began, Della worried she wouldn't be able to stop. This must be how Katrin had felt when she started at Ruthersfield, missing her home in Iceland with no one being very nice to her.

"Full moon," someone murmured from across the room. "Witches will be out tonight, hexing the crops, turning the milk sour, riding the salmon up the river."

Della let out a choking laugh. That was such a ridiculous thing to say. Witches just liked full moons because it was easier to fly at night. These people didn't know the first thing about being a witch, Della realized, any more than Melanie knew the first thing about being from Iceland. In fact none of the girls had bothered to ask Katrin what her home was actually like. She must have felt so sad and misunderstood, and Della wished she'd been more of a friend.

"Witches are no joking matter," another voice whispered through the gloom. "My mother's cousin's uncle saw one with his own eyes, sitting on a giant mushroom in the forest, casting her evil spells. Chased her with a stick, he did, but she turned into a bird and flew away."

"Witches are not evil," Della whispered under her breath, but softly so no one could hear. A rat ran by, and she gave a muffled squeal. Right now all she wanted was to get back home, where witches were considered national treasures, where they were respected and admired and invited to Buckingham Palace for fancy teas. And the only way to do that was the travel amulet, which she felt quite certain Tom

Foolery had. So, since he refused to give it to her, she would just have to steal it back.

The next morning Della asked Mrs. Chambers if she could possibly work in the castle and not the kitchen because of her finger. "It's difficult to chop with," Della said. "And I don't want to cut myself again."

"Humph. I suppose," Mrs. Chambers agreed rather grumpily. "Although his lordship was looking forward to more of your pheasant stew."

"I will make it again," Della promised.

"You can sweep the floors, put down fresh rushes, and see about making beds," Mrs. Chambers muttered. "William will be in charge of you over there."

William, it turned out, was the person who had opened the door to her when she first arrived. He was rather like a butler, Della thought, giving out orders but not doing any of the work himself.

Sweeping the dirt and trampled rushes out of one corridor took over an hour, and Della realized that if she was going to use her time to hunt for the travel amulet, she would have to speed things up. Honestly, these people had no idea how much easier their lives would be with a little bit of magic. Della started sweeping the great hall, waiting for William and a group of knights to leave, and as soon as they did, she pulled out her wand and cast a quick tidy up spell. "Tidylisious," Della murmured, waving her beech stick around. The jolt of magic was so strong she dropped her wand, the hairs on her arms standing up. "A little gentler next time," Della gasped, watching the rushes blow themselves into a heap by the door. But it was worth it, because all she had to do was sweep the pile outside. Now she could hunt for Tom Foolery's room.

Heading up the main staircase, Della found herself standing in the gallery that overlooked the great hall. This was where the musicians played at mealtimes. There were doors leading off it, and peeking inside one, Della saw that these were the bedchambers. The largest one, with tapestry wall hangings and an ornate four-poster bed, had to be Lord and Lady Hepworth's room. The other rooms were smaller, and rather plain, and it was hard to tell if Tom Foolery slept in any of them.

Keeping an eye out for people, Della cast the same tidying spell in each chamber, remembering not to wave her stick so dramatically. This seemed to keep the magic from shooting out in a great rush, and it was very satisfying to watch the mattresses stand up and give themselves a good shake and the covers roll smoothly into place. Della stood by the door while the old rushes blew out of the narrow windows, and a fresh straw covering blew in, looking from outside like nothing more than a strong wind. Since there was a faint whiff of unwashed bodies up here, too, Della cast a lavender-scented spell over each of the rooms so the subtle fragrance lingered in the air.

At the end of the corridor, Della discovered a narrow door with a spiral staircase behind it. She climbed up, breathing in the musty dampness, and stepped out into another hallway. This looked more promising, and Della knew she was close, because she could hear Tom Foolery singing. Following the noise, Della tiptoed along the passage, stopping outside a room with the door open a crack. Peering through, she could just make out the jester, juggling a handful of what looked like sticks tied with ribbons. Della stood quite still, but he glanced up, as if sensing something, and looked over at the door. She stepped back quickly, hoping he hadn't seen her. Closing her eyes for a moment, Della took a deep breath before creeping away. At least now she knew where his room was. And the second he left, she planned to go in and find her necklace.

Chapter Fourteen

In Which Ivan Draws a Picture

NOT WANTING TO GO BACK DOWNSTAIRS, DELLA TIP-
toed along the corridor, deciding to wait around
until Tom Foolery left his room. She had time to spare.
The cleaning was done, and it seemed unlikely that
anyone would come looking for her.

Right at the end of the passage was a door, and
Della opened it as quietly as possible, deciding to hide
in there so she wouldn't be discovered loitering in the
hallway. She slipped inside, startled to find Ivan sitting on a stool by the window. He had a piece of paper
spread across his knees and appeared to be sketching.
Wood shavings were scattered around his feet, and a

number of carvings were clustered on the deep stone sill of the narrow window.

"What are you doing up here?" Della whispered. "You gave me a shock."

"I could ask you the same question."

"I've been cleaning the castle." She held up her hand. "Since I cut my finger, Mrs. Chambers said I didn't have to be around knives."

Ivan grinned. "So you were exploring?"

"Sort of," Della confessed.

"Well, I'm hiding," Ivan admitted. "From my father. I'm supposed to be out there practicing my jousting, and I don't want to do it. So this is where I come to escape. Here or the river."

"You like to draw as well as carve?" Della asked, walking across the room.

Ivan shrugged. "I enjoy it. I'm not sure how good I am."

Della pointed at a canvas that was propped on the floor facing the wall. "Is that one of yours?"

"Oh, no." Ivan shook his head. "Definitely not. We don't look at him anymore."

"Him? It's your father?" Della said, turning the picture around and seeing the red, bearded face of Lord Hepworth.

"That's not my father. It's his brother, James. His twin."

"And we don't look at him because . . . ?"

"Because he tried to run a sword through my father and take the castle for himself."

"Not very brotherly behavior," Della murmured, looking at the portrait with its thick layers of paint.

"He was born second, which means he didn't inherit the main estate. That goes to the oldest son. When my grandfather died, James, my uncle, got a pig farm that the family owns in the Highlands of Scotland, and my father got Castle Hepworth and twenty thousand acres of land, including all the surrounding villages."

"Well, I have to admit that doesn't seem very fair."

Ivan gave her a strange look. "It's the law, Della. And not only did he try to slay my father, he threatened to burn the castle and Potts Bottom to the ground."

Della turned the picture back against the wall. "Okay, I agree. Not a nice man."

"Where exactly are you from?" Ivan asked, giving her a quizzical look. "I'm not sure what it is about you, but you say things in a different way."

"It's a long story," Della sighed, walking over to stand by the window. She didn't look at Ivan as she spoke, because it was hard to lie and make eye contact. "The short version is I've got relatives in Potts Bottom I was meant to be visiting, but when I arrived here, they had left. So I'm working to get money to go home again." There was some truth in this story. She did have relatives in Potts Bottom, her family, although they wouldn't be born for another eight centuries, but it was the best (and most believable) answer she could come up with.

Wanting to change the subject, Della nodded at what looked to be a burnt stick in Ivan's hand. He hadn't started to sketch anything yet, but his fingers were stained black from holding it. "What is that?"

"Willow twig. I bundle them up and take them to the baker's at the end of the day, and he leaves them in his oven for me overnight. They make excellent drawing sticks."

"That's so clever," Della said, realizing this was an early form of charcoal.

"Can I draw you?" Ivan suddenly asked. "I get tired of always copying this view. It would be nice to have a person to draw."

"Well . . ." Della hesitated, feeling self-conscious. But she did want to stay up here until Tom Foolery left his room, and this was a perfect excuse. "Okay. If you like."

"Stand just where you are, by the window," Ivan said, starting to sketch. "This is about the only place in the castle that gets good sunlight."

Della glanced through the window, seeing the village of Potts Bottom spread below her. Except there was no canal or bustling town center, and if her sense of direction was correct (which it very well might not be), there was a field of sheep where Ruthersfield Academy should be.

"What's wrong?" Ivan asked. "You look so sad."

"I miss my home," Della said, swallowing hard. "I really miss it."

Ivan didn't ask any more questions, which was nice, because she knew if he did, she would cry. And standing there quietly gave her time to collect herself. She could feel the sun on her face through the tiny window and smell real fresh air that didn't need to be perfumed with magic.

"You like doing things with your hands, don't you?" Della said softly. "I do too."

"I can tell you have a way with the animals," Ivan said. "You've got a gentle touch, Della."

"That isn't exactly a skill."

"It's a gift."

"So is what you do."

"But it's not courageous, is it, playing about with wood and drawing pictures." Ivan flicked his gaze up at her. "You probably think I'm a coward."

"No, I don't at all. I think you're really talented. Your carvings are incredible, Ivan."

"I am a coward. I don't want to joust and knock

people off their horses. I don't want to risk my life for the sake of my honor and looking brave."

"Then I'm a coward too, because I'd hate to do those things."

Ivan smiled at her and held up the sketch. "There. What do you think?"

"I think . . ." Della tilted her head to one side, scrambling for something to say. "It's . . ." She cleared her throat and tried again. "It's . . ."

"You seem lost for words," Ivan said. "Don't you think I have captured your likeness?"

"Ivan!" Della burst out laughing. "I'm sorry." She giggled. "It's just that I look like a middle-aged woman. A grumpy middle-aged woman."

"You're supposed to look wistful," Ivan said, examining his artwork.

"And please tell me I don't have a nose that big."

"I haven't done many portraits," Ivan admitted. "I usually draw landscapes." He studied the picture and then looked up at Della. "It isn't my best work, I'll admit."

"Doesn't matter, if you enjoy it," Della said, not suggesting that he should probably stick to carving, because she didn't want to hurt his feelings. "I should go. I'm supposed to be cleaning rooms."

"I should too," Ivan sighed. "Before my father comes

looking for me." But he didn't move, and as Della opened the door, he said, "I understand you want to go home, Della, but you should know I'm glad you're here. It's nice having a friend in the castle."

"Yes, it is," Della agreed, smiling at Ivan before slipping out into the hallway.

She couldn't hear singing as she crept up to Tom Foolery's door. Pressing her ear against it, Della held her breath and listened, but it was completely quiet. No rustling or noise at all. She waited another few moments and then gently pressed down the latch. It didn't open, and Della pressed again, harder this time. She rattled the handle and pushed her weight against the door, but Tom Foolery had clearly locked it. Which shouldn't have come as a surprise, although Della couldn't help banging the wall in frustration. And of course she didn't know any breaking-and-entering spells, because they didn't learn that kind of magic at Ruthersfield. If you were caught doing something like that, you'd have your license to practice magic taken away. *But I bet Dame Bessie knows a good unlocking spell,* Della thought. This definitely counted as survival magic. And when they met at Dame Bessie's cottage in three nights' time, Della was determined to find out what spell she could use to break into Tom Foolery's room.

Chapter Fifteen

A Courage Potion Is Brewed

GETTING OUT OF THE CASTLE ON WEDNESDAY NIGHT was easy. Nobody seemed too bothered by Della's whereabouts, so she simply waited until the kitchen was full of snoring and then slipped outside to get her branch from behind the stables. "Avante, and please keep me from crashing," Della whispered, taking off with a lurch. She flew straight up behind the castle, gripping the branch in her sweaty hands. When she had gained as much height as she could cope with, she circled back around to fly over the forest. The wind was much stronger up here, and Della clung on tight, doing her best not to look down. She had to reach for her wand when she thought Dame Bessie's cottage should be coming into view, and cast an illumination spell to light up the end. This way she could see the tiny cottage tucked in a clearing below her. Della would not have scored points for her landing from Ms. Durkin, their flying teacher, but this wasn't Ruthersfield, and good landing posture didn't matter right now. Getting inside without being discovered did.

Bralin and Tambor were sitting on the gateposts, and as she hurried past, they let out a soft cry. To announce her arrival, Della guessed, because before she got up to the door, it was cracked open, and Dame Bessie beckoned her inside. Willow, Faye, and Isolda were already there. And Gwyneth, too, of course, since she was staying with Dame Bessie. But not Mary.

"I hope she's all right." Della fretted, bending down to give Gwyneth a hug. "She's only seven. That's far too young to be flying by herself."

"It's the safest way here," Dame Bessie said, but Della could tell she was worried too by the way she kept glancing out of the window. And both Della and Dame Bessie rushed for the door when Tambor and Bralin gave their low cry.

Mary was sobbing as she burst into the room. "I almost f-f-fell off my branch, and my m-mother found purple f-flowers floating in the pottage after I had stirred it."

"Must have been the spoon you were using," Dame Bessie said. "You have to be careful, Mary. Certain woods will stir up your magic if you touch them."

"I'm s-scared," Mary sobbed. "I don't want to fly ever again. I don't want to be a witch anymore."

"Now take a breath and calm down, child," Dame Bessie said. "Remember how to turn into a mouse or a rat? In case you need to get away."

"Not a snail?" Mary said, sniffing.

"No, a snail probably wouldn't be fast enough," Della murmured, putting her arm around Mary. "Why don't we make you some courage potion? Then you won't need to be so frightened anymore."

"You can make a courage potion?" Dame Bessie questioned Della. "I've never come across such a spell before."

"It's a good survival technique," Della pointed out. "Channeling your inner courage. We use it all the time where I come from." The girls often took courage potions before a math quiz or tryouts for the broomstick-gymnastics team. "If Mary feels brave, it will help her stay calm, which will help keep her magic under control," Della reasoned. "So she'll have less chance of being discovered."

"Interesting," Dame Bessie said. "Sounds like something we could all make use of. I would like to see how you brew one." She pointed her wand at the fireplace, and just like before, the stone hearth opened up, exposing the narrow flight of stairs. One by one the girls followed Dame Bessie down into her workroom. She led them over to a shelf full of dusty stone bottles, none of which appeared to be labeled, so it was difficult to know what was what.

"Now, tell me what you need, my dear, and I can see if I have it."

"Okay, let me just think for a minute. I want to be sure I get it right. Condensed dragon's breath is the main ingredient," Della said, the girls looking at her with interest. "There is a courage potion that calls for powdered griffin's tooth, but dragon's breath works much better. And a lion's roar. Although if you don't have one of those, you can substitute any fierce roar. Then just a little crushed hawthorn and bayberry."

"This, and this," Dame Bessie murmured, opening and sniffing and taking bottles off the shelf. "And would a troll roar do? I have no lion."

"I'm sure it will be fine," Della said, wondering where Dame Bessie got her ingredients, because she certainly wasn't ordering them from *The Witches' Supply Catalogue*.

"I gather them myself," Dame Bessie said, as if she could read Della's mind, which maybe she could, Della thought, since mind reading was an ancient magic that didn't get banned until the 1700s.

"Have you ever met a dragon?" Mary asked, wide-eyed.

"Not personally, but if you go out in the early hours during the winter months, you can see their breath clinging to the tops of the leaves. It's easy enough to collect."

"And a troll roar?" Della couldn't help asking.

"They bellow so loud you can hear them throughout the forest. Just open a bottle and in it goes."

Dame Bessie's cellar was not like the potions room at Ruthersfield. No clean glass beakers and sterilized equipment to mix the courage potion in. Della had to use a rather dirty-looking wooden bowl, crushing the hawthorn berries with a stone. When she shook in the troll roar, it bellowed out a medieval obscenity, and the girls giggled, covering their mouths in shock. Threads of tangerine smoke curled out of the bowl, accompanied by a great deal of hissing and bubbling.

Picking up a black feather quill, Dame Bessie bent over the table and dipped the sharp end in a pot of ink. Then, repeating the spell under her breath, she carefully wrote down what Della was doing. "So I don't forget," Dame Bessie murmured. "There are empty bottles at the end of the shelf, Della. Divide the potion out and give everyone some to take home."

"I shall drink mine before I fly back," Mary said. "I feel braver already, and I haven't even had any."

"I'm going to save mine until another witch gets caught," Willow announced. "That's when I get most frightened, thinking I'll be next."

"We can always make more," Dame Bessie said, "now that Della has shown us how. But in case any of you do get caught . . ." She paused here a moment and looked around at the girls. "Well, that's why I'm going to teach you how to wipe such knowledge right out of a person's mind. We can't practice this, of course, but you should know what to do if the situation arises. Now listen carefully." The girls stared at her in somber silence, except for Gwyneth, who was leaning against Della, rubbing her eyes. "With a steady hand point your wand at whoever has discovered your identity," Dame Bessie continued, "and then in a clear voice say the word 'wipplelashwitch.'"

"Wipplelashwitch," Della whispered, thinking that this could be quite useful, and then amazed that she was actually considering the possibility of using such a spell. But her life had changed, and sitting around crying over it wasn't going to get her back home. She had to do everything she could to survive. "Dame Bessie, you don't know any good unlocking spells, do you?"

Della asked, imagining that Ms. Cray would wash her mouth out with unicorn soap if she heard her asking such a question.

"Indeed I do," Dame Bessie replied. And Della listened carefully to every word Dame Bessie said, learning exactly how to break into Tom Foolery's room. She could feel her pulse starting to race at the thought of carrying out such a plan and slipped the little bottle of courage potion into her pocket, knowing she was definitely going to need it later on.

Chapter Sixteen

....

A Surprise Meeting

"ARE YOU GOING TO BE OKAY GETTING HOME?" DELLA asked Mary as they collected their branches from the woodpile.

"I don't feel scared at all," Mary announced, swigging the last of her courage potion. She gave a loud, troll-like burp and, with a quick wave at Della, soared off into the night.

The sky had cleared while they were at Dame Bessie's, and as Della flew over the castle, she could just make out a number of knights on watch duty. Perhaps there had been talk of another witch sighting, and not wanting to risk being seen, Della headed toward the cluster of trees by the river. She glided down, managing to stay in control until the last moment, when she landed in a heap on the bank. "Ouch!" Della lay still for a minute, making sure nothing hurt before getting gingerly to her feet.

It was as she rubbed her elbow that she saw the figure watching her, standing a few yards away at the edge of the trees. Catching her breath, Della froze. Very slowly she felt for her wand, never believing she would have to use the spell she had just learned quite so soon. But if someone had seen her flying, she would need to wipe that memory clean. Although when the person spoke her name, she realized with a shock it was Ivan.

"Della?" he said, keeping his distance. "Did you . . . ? Were you . . . ?" Ivan's voice petered away, as if he couldn't say the words out loud.

"Ivan, please, it's not like you think it is. . . ." Della knew she should simply erase the memory from his mind, before she lost her nerve. But he was her friend. He'd confided in her and drawn her picture, and she just couldn't do it.

"You're a witch?"

"I am, but I'm not evil. I've never done anything evil in my life," Della said, leaving the wand in her pocket. "Where I come from, Ivan, people aren't frightened of witches. In fact they love them."

Ivan put his hand on his sword. "Why didn't you tell me this before?"

"Because I don't want to end up in your dungeon," Della said. "I just want to go home."

"Then why not fly home? What's keeping you here?"

"I've lost something very special," Della said. "And I can't leave until I find it." She took a deep breath to stop her voice from trembling. "Which is what I was trying to do now," she added, feeling like an explanation for her midnight flying was needed.

"And did you? Find it?"

"No, but I'm close. I know where it is, and I think I know how to get it. But what are you doing out here?" Della said, deciding it was time to move the conversation away from witches.

Ivan didn't answer, and it was too dark to see his expression. "I'm running away," he finally said. "But you probably know that because you're a witch and you can read my thoughts."

"Oh don't be ridiculous. Of course I can't, and even if I could read your thoughts, I wouldn't. In my country that's completely illegal."

"Since all I do is disappoint my father, I think it's better if I go," Ivan said, starting to walk away. Della could see he was limping, and she hurried after him.

"You can't go anywhere like that."

Ivan sped up and stumbled, looking back at Della in fear.

"Oh stop acting like I'm going to turn you into a toad," she said impatiently. "What did you do?"

"I fell," Ivan admitted. "And I've cut my leg."

"That's what comes from running away at night," Della muttered. She crouched down beside him and saw that his pantaloons, or tights or whatever he called them, were ripped, and a nasty gash had bled through the fabric. "You're a mess."

"Can you stitch me up?" Ivan said. "I have a rag I can bite on while you sew."

"That is such a horrid image." Della shuddered and reached for her wand.

"No! Please don't hurt me." Ivan flinched, shielding his face with his arm.

"Oh will you stop that. This won't hurt one bit," Della said. She waved the wand over Ivan's leg. "Healitoesious!" Della whispered, and in the faint glow of moonlight watched the cut knit itself back together.

"Unbelievable," Ivan gasped, running a hand across the wound. "It's gone."

"See, magic is a good thing," Della said. "If everyone here would stop being so hysterical about witches, they might see that."

"Except there's talk tonight about a young witch on

the far side of Giddington who stirred up a wind strong enough to blow down three of the houses in the village."

"Probably because she doesn't know how to control her magic," Della snapped. "Or maybe she's so frustrated she couldn't help calling up a wind. I mean, what do you expect? If you can't be yourself and you're always trying to hide who you really are and everyone hates you just because you're different. That is not easy, Ivan." Della stared at him, breathing hard. "Witches are not these awful, evil creatures who fly about putting hexes on everyone."

"Yes, I can see that," Ivan said, glancing around. "But no one else does, so you should keep your voice down, Della. If my father's knights find out what you are, they will throw you straight in the dungeon."

"You're right. I'm sorry," Della said, realizing she had to be more careful. It wasn't her job to change these people's minds. That was up to Witch Dupree, and good luck to her, Della thought. Besides, she didn't want to get Ivan into trouble by being caught talking to a witch.

"I'd better be going," he sighed.

"But where to? You can't just go chasing off without a plan."

"Back home." Ivan shook back his hair. "My mother

would miss me, and it's a coward's way out. I'm not a coward, Della, so I shall get on my horse and joust."

"Here," Della said, impulsively pulling the little bottle of courage potion out of her pocket. "Drink this before the competition, Ivan. It won't help you win, but it will give you the courage you need to fight."

"Magic?" Ivan asked a little cautiously.

"Good magic," Della pointed out, deciding that Ivan needed the courage potion far more than she did.

Chapter Seventeen

....

A Different Kind of Magic

OVER THE NEXT FEW DAYS POOR DELLA COULDN'T find a time to slip away from Mrs. Chambers's steely presence. With guests arriving for the jousting tournament, Della was kept busy in the kitchen, plucking birds for roasting over the fire and stirring the bubbling pans of pottage, but the worst job of all was the fish she had to pickle in big barrels of sour, salty brine so pungent it made her eyes water. Every time Della tried to escape from the kitchen, Mrs. Chambers would give her a new job.

"These are important guests," Mrs. Chambers kept

muttering, handing Della a pile of preserved plums to chop.

Della could hear the carriages arriving, rumbling over the cobblestones, and as she lugged water back from the well, it was difficult not to stare at the elegantly dressed ladies getting out of them. A steady stream of knights paraded around the castle, throwing their cloaks over puddles so the women wouldn't get their shoes wet and generally trying to outdo each other with their lavish displays of chivalry.

"Lord Hepworth has requested that you make your special pottage for tonight's feast," Mrs. Chambers instructed.

"Shall I help clean the rooms first?" Della said, desperate to find the travel amulet. She had been tied to the kitchen for five days now, and there were so many guests milling about that slipping away upstairs seemed next to impossible.

"Pheasant stew," Mrs. Chambers ordered, "and it better be as good as before."

Della picked up a spoon, dropping it quickly back on the table.

"And what is the matter now?" Mrs. Chambers barked, shaking her head at Della. "I don't know what's got into you lately. Jumpy as a jackrabbit, you are."

"Sorry." Della reached for the spoon again. This time she was prepared for the tingling that shot through her fingers. Beech wood, Della realized.

"And I don't know what's so funny," Mrs. Chambers added, glaring at Della's smile. "There's work to be done."

"I'm just glad that Lord Hepworth likes my stew," Della said, happy that whipping up a chicken curry was going to be a whole lot easier than she'd anticipated. Instead of getting out her wand, she could just use the spoon. It was long and narrow at one end, and should conduct spells just as well as a beech stick.

Della waited until Mrs. Chambers had bustled off to the pantry before waving the spoon over the soup pot. There was so much activity going on in the kitchen that no one paid much attention to the cloud of orange smoke. Tasting a bit, Della had to admit that the flavor was a little different from the last curry spell, sweeter, with extra-plump raisins floating in it, and she hoped that Lord Hepworth would approve.

Much to Della's delight, Lord Hepworth not only approved, but was so pleased by the compliments the stew received from his guests that he invited Della and the rest of the kitchen staff in to watch Tom Foolery perform.

"Now, no talking, and stand well back," Mrs. Chambers whispered, herding them into the great hall.

An enormous fire burned in the hearth, and the tables were crowded with people. Della spied Ivan squeezed in between his father and a pale girl in a blue velvet dress who kept fanning herself. She had pearls woven through her hair and looked like the sort of damsel in distress who might easily be in need of rescuing. Since she was obviously very busy fluttering her eyes at the knight on her other side, Ivan was able to whittle away at a piece of wood without anyone noticing, except for Della, who could see the little knife in his hand.

"Attention, everyone," Lord Hepworth called out, waiting for the noise to subside. "For your pleasure and entertainment, I give you Tom Foolery."

The guests erupted in a chorus of cheering and clapping as the jester bounded into the room, cartwheeling his way across the floor and bowing to the crowd. He shook his bells and danced over to the table, skipping along and pulling flowers out of the ladies' hair. They oohed and aahed and clapped again as he gave another bow, offering the flowers to Lady Hepworth, who looked magnificent in a rose-colored, lace-trimmed gown.

"He is good, isn't he?" Myrtle whispered.

Leaning over the table, Tom Foolery cut into one of the pies, and a flock of blackbirds flew out, causing the crowd to gasp in amazement. Then he waved his hands over a large roasted pike. The fish flapped its tail on the platter, and the girl in the blue velvet dress squealed in horror. Della had noticed a thin thread tied around the fish's tail in the kitchen, and now she could tell Tom Foolery was pulling it.

"It's clever, but it's not magic," Della said softly, thinking how unfair it was that the jester could perform his kind of tricks, but witches weren't allowed to practice real magic. She noticed Tom Foolery staring at her, a bitter look on his face, and Della wondered if he'd been able to read her lips. Although why he should seem so upset, she had no idea.

Myrtle gave a horrified gasp. "Of course it's not magic," she hissed. "Don't even say such a word out loud."

"I have to get out of here," Della said, suddenly feeling like she couldn't breathe.

"It is rather hot," Myrtle agreed. "Take some fresh air."

"Fresh air." Della stared at Myrtle. "Yes . . . yes, I will." And grabbing this sudden opportunity, she added, "I'll just step outside. I'll—I'll be right back." But Della hoped, as she crept out of the hall and softly up the stairs, that she wouldn't be back at all.

Chapter Eighteen

....

An Interesting Discovery

DELLA DIDN'T NEED TO USE THE UNLOCKING SPELL she had learned from Dame Bessie, because the door to Tom Foolery's room was open. Glancing around to make sure she was still alone up here, Della quickly slipped inside. Without wasting a second, she started to search, although there weren't too many places to look. She opened a heavy wooden trunk, feeling through the folded clothes and blankets, but there was no travel amulet in there. Della moved over to the straw sleeping pallet and ran her hands underneath it, touching nothing more exciting than a thick layer of dust. A jacket and tunic thing hung on wooden pegs, but her necklace wasn't in any of the pockets. The longer she was in the room the faster Della's heart beat, until it was racing at such a speed she had to stop for a moment and take a few deep breaths, reminding herself that Tom Foolery was still safely downstairs entertaining the guests. She had time, and Della hurried over to a cupboard in the corner of the room. This looked promising, and she opened the doors, wincing as they creaked. There wasn't much on the shelves, just a basket of ribbons, a pair of soft gloves, playing cards, and a chessboard. But the thing Della's eyes were immediately drawn to was a large crystal ball, sitting on a carved wooden stand.

She glanced back over her shoulder, and her palms started to sweat. What on earth was Tom Foolery doing with a crystal ball? Della reached out a hand and lightly touched the surface. The crystal immediately began to pulse with a soft purple glow. She inhaled sharply and wiped her hands down her skirt before lifting the ball out. Cradling it carefully, she watched the center fill with a thick purple fog. Her legs had started to shake, and Della leaned against the cupboard for support, certain that Tom Foolery must have stolen this, too. He wasn't a witch, so how could he possibly own a crystal ball? Clearly Dame Bessie had been right about his magpie nature, hoarding beautiful, sparkly things that didn't belong to him.

As she stared into the center of the globe, the fog began to clear, and Della could see a picture forming. Hills and a river came into view and what looked like a gathering of men—knights, or an army of some sort. There were tethered horses and some crude-looking tents. Following the method Ms. Randal had taught them, Della focused on the thing she wanted to study in more detail, and the picture narrowed in on the men, as if she were looking through a zoom lens. At first Della thought it was Lord Hepworth, huddled around a campfire with his knights, but Lord Hepworth was downstairs drinking ale, and Della realized with a start that this must be his twin brother, James. The one who had inherited the Scottish pig farm. The one who tried to slay Lord Hepworth because he wanted the castle for himself. Crystal balls show the viewer what is important to them, and Della stared at the picture, trying to make sense of what she was seeing. The lord's brother was drawing in the dirt with a stick, a circle here, a square there, and a line running between the two. He kept pointing at the shapes as if discussing some sort of plan, and it occurred to Della with a sickening feeling that maybe he was plotting an attack. An attack on Castle Hepworth. Why else would she be shown this picture? Della swallowed down her panic, but her thoughts were spinning out of control. What if the line was the river running north of the valley, and they were somewhere on the other side of it? The square had to be Castle Hepworth. And she became even more certain when the lord's brother clenched his fist in the air, displaying the ring on his left middle finger stamped with the Hepworth crest, a dragon and two crossed swords.

"No," Della whispered. This was all getting way out of hand. She had to tell someone, but who? Not Lord Hepworth, who probably wouldn't believe her anyway, especially once he discovered she was a witch. Because how else could she have seen what she had seen? It would have to be Ivan.

Della was just putting the crystal ball back in the cupboard when the door opened behind her. She jerked around, giving a frightened gasp as Tom Foolery walked into the room.

"Wh-wh-what?" the jester spluttered, striding toward her. Anger flashed across his face. "What are you doing in here?" The crystal ball was still glowing purple, and Della slammed the cupboard shut. "Have you been trifling with my things?" the jester hissed.

"I—I . . ." Della's voice dried up. He didn't like her, that was clear, and she couldn't think straight, worrying about what he had seen. There was nothing she could say that Tom Foolery might believe. Certainly not that she was in here to clean. "I was looking for my necklace," she said at last.

"And did you find it?"

"No," Della croaked, beginning to wonder if maybe she'd been wrong about him. Maybe he hadn't taken it after all. Which right now was even more upsetting than confronting an angry jester, because it meant that the necklace really was lost.

"Anything else I can do for you?" Tom Foolery said, staring at her so hard Della was sure he knew what she'd been doing.

Della shook her head, her mouth dry, and before Tom Foolery could ask her any more questions, she bolted from the room.

Chapter Nineteen

....

The Rat Visitor

IVAN WAS STILL AT THE TABLE WHEN DELLA CAME BACK down, and it looked like he was going to be trapped there for some time, considering the noise and laughter and amount of ale being drunk.

"There you are, child," Mrs. Chambers said, loading Della's arms with empty platters and sweeping her off to the kitchen. "Myrtle said you needed air. Are you feeling better?"

"Not really," Della admitted. "I feel a bit faint." Which was an understatement. She had never felt more shaky or scared in her life. What had Tom Foolery seen, and would he say anything to Lord Hepworth? This was worrying enough, but even worse was the fear that Lord Hepworth's brother might be, right this very second, charging toward the castle. And as the evening wore on, Della got more and more frantic, because she couldn't find a way to get Ivan alone so she could tell him.

"I must do something," Della fretted under her breath, scrubbing the kitchen table. And even though she knew she shouldn't interfere with history, she decided to confide in Dame Bessie. Della couldn't keep this information to herself, and Dame Bessie would know what to do. The girls were meeting tonight anyway, so perhaps they could all weave a protective web around the castle, or put up an invisible wall that would keep invaders out. It was also time to explain where she had really come from, because Dame Bessie was the only person (apart from the no-show Witch Dupree) who might possibly be able to help her get back now.

As Della lay on her mat waiting to slip out, she could hear the rats scrabbling about under the table, searching for scraps of food. One of them scurried right up to Della and sniffed at her hair. By the light from the fire she could see a pair of pale, watery-blue eyes staring at her. The creature studied Della with a strange focus, not looking away or blinking or acting like a normal rat at all. Something about the animal seemed extremely familiar, especially the way it was looking at her.

"Mary?" she whispered softly. "Is that you?"

The rat nuzzled Della's neck and gave what was undeniably a sort of nod. A cold, sick feeling settled in Della's stomach. Something bad must have happened, and she couldn't lie here a second longer. There was no time to waste. She had to get to Dame Bessie's. Della opened her pocket, and without hesitating, the rat crawled inside.

Trying not to make a noise, Della got slowly to her feet.

"And where are you going, girl?" Mrs. Chambers called out. "I hear you shuffling over there."

"I still feel a bit sick," Della whispered. "I just need a little fresh air."

"Well, don't go far," Mrs. Chambers murmured. "It's the witching hour, and you don't know who's about."

The moon was bright, and a silvery glow flooded the courtyard. Della crept over to the stables, and as soon as she was behind them, she squatted down and whispered, "You can come out now, Mary."

The rat scuttled onto the ground and sat in front of Della. "Don't change back yet," Della whispered. "It's safer this way. Wait till we get to Dame Bessie's." Mary stared hard at Della, keeping her gaze focused, and all of a sudden Della could hear Mary's voice in her head. She looked around to see if anyone else had spoken, but it definitely sounded like Mary, and it definitely wasn't coming from outside. "I think I can understand what you're saying," Della whispered, "and of course you're scared, Mary. Can you tell me what happened?" Did being back here in medieval times make her more open to this sort of magic, Della wondered, because clear as day it was as if Mary was talking to her.

"My brothers saw me flying." Mary kept her eyes fixed on Della's face. "I was sweeping the floor with a new broom Pa had bought at the Deckle Mead market. Halfway across the room it started twitching, and before I could let go, it had lifted me into the air."

"I bet it was made of cherry wood," Della said softly. "Isn't that the one you had a strong reaction to?"

Mary nodded, her whiskers quivering. "They just stood there," Della could hear her saying, "mouths hanging open, staring at me. And not knowing what else to do, the second I came down I turned into a rat and ran away."

"Oh, Mary," Della whispered, stroking the rat's soft fur. "I'm so sorry."

"I should have taken the memory out of their heads, but there were two of them, and I got scared. . . ."

"Of course you did," Della murmured, thinking that

if anyone saw her talking to a rat, they would believe she was insane. "But it's not too late," Della whispered. "Dame Bessie will figure out what to do. I promise it's going to be fine, Mary." Although Della knew she shouldn't be promising anything of the sort. Especially when she looked for her beech branch and discovered that it wasn't there. "I had a feeling this was going to happen, but did it have to be tonight?" Della fretted, hunting around in a panic. But the branch had definitely gone. Probably burned in the kitchen fire by now.

"We're going to have to walk, Mary," Della said, trying to keep her voice steady.

The rat's eyes swam with fear. "What if they're out looking for me?"

"No one will see you," Della whispered, picking Mary up and putting her gently in her pocket. "It's going to be fun, an adventure," she added, except there was nothing fun about this at all.

As Della walked over the drawbridge, she could feel the warm weight of Mary pressing against her. It was actually rather comforting, having a small furry creature tucked up in her pocket again.

"Who goes there?" a gruff voice demanded, and one of Lord Hepworth's knights loomed up in front of her.

"I—I work at the castle," Della said, desperately trying to think of what to say. The guard towered above her, and in the silvery light Della could see the metal glint of his sword. "I'm off to pick night mushrooms for the lord's breakfast," she blurted out.

"Night mushrooms?"

"Yes, of course. You must know that you can only pick them when the moon is bright. Otherwise they won't have the flavor." Della couldn't believe she had said something quite so ridiculous, but it was too late to change her story now.

The guard looked puzzled. "You're the one that makes that pheasant stew?"

"I am, and you wait till you taste my fried night mushrooms," Della said. "You have heard of night mushrooms, I presume?" She looked straight up at the knight, even though her mouth was dry and her palms were damp.

"Of course I have." The knight nodded somberly. "A rare delicacy indeed." He waved Della past, and with Mary in her pocket, she hurried as fast as she could toward Dame Bessie's.

Chapter Twenty

· ·

Things Get Dramatically Worse

FINDING HER WAY THROUGH THE WOOD WASN'T EASY, especially when Della was used to approaching Dame Bessie's by air. She kept stopping to listen, sure that she could hear twigs snapping behind her, but whenever she froze and held her breath, the only sound Della heard was the soft distant hoot of an owl. It was a relief to finally see the dark shapes of Tambor and Bralin sitting on the gateposts, still as statues, keeping watch over the night. Della stroked Tambor's head as she walked through the gate, glancing back at a scuffle of leaves.

"Probably just an animal," Della whispered, straining her ears. She was so anxious, of course she was hearing noises.

Dame Bessie could tell something was wrong the second she opened the door. Della burst inside, but before she could speak, Dame Bessie put a finger against her lips. "Remember, the forest has ears."

The second Dame Bessie closed the door, Della exploded, "I don't know what to do, Dame Bessie," filling her in on the crystal ball she had found and the vision she was sure she had seen. "What if I'm right, and Lord Hepworth's brother is planning to attack the castle?"

"Then we have a catastrophe on our hands," Dame Bessie pronounced soberly. She glanced at the door. "We must go downstairs to talk. You go on ahead, Della. I'll wait for Mary to get here."

"Oh, I almost forgot. Mary is here," Della said, opening up her pocket. The little rat was curled in a ball, snoring away softly. "Her brothers caught her floating from a broom, and she didn't know what else to do."

Dame Bessie nodded. "Don't wake the poor child. She's going to have to face this soon enough." The old woman had just pulled out her wand and opened up the staircase when Tambor and Bralin started shrieking. "What in the world?" Dame Bessie said, but before she had time to find out who had disturbed the birds, the cottage door was shoved open, and in stormed a cluster of knights.

"In the name of King Henry, you are all under arrest." One of the knights grabbed Della by the arm. "Wicked creatures! Don't even attempt to put me under a hex."

"I don't know any hexes," Della cried, trying to pull away.

Keeping a tight grip on her, the knight held out his free hand. "Give me your magic stick," he demanded.

Seeing no escape, Della pulled the wand from her pocket. The knight broke it in half and threw the pieces on the fire. Dame Bessie's wand followed, and Della watched in horror as Willow, Faye, Gwyneth, and Isolda were marched up the stairs by two more knights.

"Found these witches in the basement," one of the knights said, giving Faye a rough prod in the back. "Casting their evil magic about."

"No we weren't," Faye cried out, and little Gwyneth started to cry.

"I want my mama," Gwyneth sobbed. "You are not nice."

The knights confiscated the rest of the wands, and with a crackle and hiss, the pile of sticks went up in flames. Heavy chains were snapped around the girls' wrists, and they were hustled outside. A cart stood in front of the cottage. Tambor and Bralin circled around it, dipping and diving and squawking in the driver's face.

"Up you go," one of the knights said, herding Dame Bessie and the girls into the back. "Filthy, stinking witches." He looked at Della in disgust. "And to think you've been hiding in the castle, right under our noses."

"I wasn't hiding," Della said, lifting her chin up and refusing to look away. She didn't know where this courage was coming from, but she couldn't stay silent any longer. Especially since she was about to be locked in a dungeon. "And we are no more filthy or stinking than you."

"His lordship is going to be most upset when he finds out he's been harboring a witch."

Della could feel Mary waking up, her little paws scrabbling about. "Stay still," she whispered. The guard stared at her, and Della pretended she was talking to Gwyneth. "It's going to be all right, Gwyneth," she said, putting her arm around the trembling girl beside her. But it wasn't all right at all. Things couldn't get much worse. And that's when Della caught a glimpse of Tom Foolery, lurking behind some trees. It was definitely the jester, his peculiar floppy hat making him look like a strange-headed beast in the moonlight. "Did you follow me?" she cried out. "It was you, wasn't it?"

Tom Foolery didn't reply.

"Why would you do this?" Della shouted. "I've never done anything terrible to you, or Lord Hepworth."

The knights mounted their horses, and the cart began to move. Some of the riders held flaming torches, and as the cart rolled past the jester, he looked up briefly. In the flickering light Della was sure she caught a flash of guilt in his eyes, but when she turned to look again he had gone.

"You haven't done anything wrong, girls," Dame Bessie said. "Just remember that." But Dame Bessie hung her head, as if she'd been defeated.

"We haven't," Della agreed. Although knowing this didn't alter the fact that they were still being taken to the castle, shackled like prisoners.

The cart trundled up the track. Della couldn't help noticing how beautiful the night was. Moonlight flooded the landscape, and it suddenly occurred to her that this might be her last time outside. Forever. Except Della didn't really believe this. Surely Lord Hepworth wouldn't lock her up. But this hope quickly faded as they crossed the drawbridge and pulled to a stop in the courtyard.

"Take them to the dungeons," Lord Hepworth ordered, standing outside the castle. Knights milled around him, and Della could see Ivan, a few feet away from the crowd. They looked at each other, and Della knew right away, there was nothing he could do.

"I'm so sorry," Ivan mouthed. He stepped toward her, but one of the knights barred his way.

"Stand back, Master Ivan. Witches are dangerous things, and you don't want to get too close."

"We are not dangerous," Della cried. "This is ridiculous."

"Who knows what evil they were plotting," the knight said.

"One at a time and don't even think about flying," another knight ordered, directing them off the cart. He kept his arms tightly folded, obviously not wanting to touch them.

"You cannot treat us this way," Dame Bessie spoke up. "What harm have we done? These girls are young and innocent, and I'm just an old woman."

"Lord Hepworth, please," Della pleaded, feeling a stick prod her in the back toward the dungeons. "You have to listen to me. Your brother has got an army together, and he's on his way to attack the castle."

"My brother's on his pig farm in Scotland," Lord Hepworth said.

"No, he's not. He's somewhere nearby on the other side of the river."

"This is an evil trick," one of the knights called out. "Don't listen to the witch, sire. She is trying to trick you so they can escape."

"Lock them up," Lord Hepworth said. "I will not be made a fool of."

"I'm not making a fool of you," Della shouted. "I'm trying to help you."

"Father, please, we should listen," Ivan said. But Della couldn't hear the rest of the conversation, because she was jostled down a dark, narrow flight of stairs and into the castle dungeons.

The walls were damp with mold, and a musty smell hung in the air.

"Get in there," one of the guards said, opening a cell and shoving the witches inside. He banged the door shut and turned a heavy iron key in the lock.

"How long do we stay here for?" Faye asked, her voice rising with panic. "I need to get home. My father and mother will be worried."

"You're not going anywhere," the guard replied, giving an enormous yawn. "Now we can all sleep easy in our beds."

"You have to believe me," Della said, stepping over to the guard. She put her hands on the bars and peered through. "I saw what's happening. Lord Hepworth's brother is coming."

"It's not going to work," the guard said. "Trying to scare us with your witchery."

"You should be scared," Della cried. But the guard was already walking away, spinning the key round his finger.

Della rested her head on the cold iron bars, beginning to understand that there was no escape. She felt sick and shaky. Her chest grew tight, and she couldn't seem to take in enough air. Not only was she never going home again, she was going to spend the rest of her life locked in this dark, miserable dungeon. And then a truly horrifying thought occurred to her. There was no Castle Hepworth in the future. What if Lord Hepworth's brother really did burn it to the ground, and because she had traveled back here and messed about with the past, she was going to get burned right along with it?

Chapter Twenty-One

·····························

Della Has a Plan

THE GIRLS SLUMPED ON THE GROUND, LEANING AGAINST one another. Della hugged Gwyneth, while Isolda and Willow rested their heads on Dame Bessie's shoulders. Faye huddled in a corner by herself. For the first time since meeting her, Della thought Dame Bessie looked old. It wasn't the wrinkles or her gray hair, but the way her eyes had lost their shine, as if the hope had leaked out of them.

"We have to do something," Della whispered, in case there were guards listening. "We can't give up. We just can't."

"This is how it goes," Dame Bessie said. "I thought I could keep you all safe. But I couldn't."

"There aren't any windows," Willow said. "Not even a tiny one."

"I can't breathe," Isolda whimpered. "Someone has to help us."

"There is no one," Della said, brushing away her tears and trying not to think about how much Gwyneth reminded her of Robbie.

Dame Bessie stared straight ahead. "I don't believe there is much we can do." Her defeat smothered the dungeon like a rain cloud, and Della could feel her own spirits sinking while the night ticked away and the dawn began to break outside. Not that they could see it, because no light shone through the cracks in the stone.

It was frightening not to have Dame Bessie take charge, telling them what to do to survive. The other girls seemed like they had already given up, their faces dull and empty. Della had never been much of a leader, but she slowly began to understand that if she didn't try to come up with a plan, no one else in here would. There had to be some way out of the dungeon—there just had to be. Perhaps they could dig a tunnel, Della thought, rubbing her fingers over the hard earth floor, except they didn't have anything to dig with. And they were all too big to squeeze through the bars. Well, maybe not all, Della suddenly realized, feeling the rat shift about in her pocket.

"Mary," she whispered in excitement. "Come up here." Mary poked her nose out and ran onto Della's lap.

"A rat!" Gwyneth shrieked, jerking away.

"Shhh. It's only Mary. We have to be quiet."

Gwyneth peeked between her fingers. "I don't like rats. Even Mary ones."

"Yes you do, because I think I have a plan, but we need Mary to be really brave and help us with it." Della stroked the little rat on the head. "Can you do that?" Mary twitched her nose. "Okay then. First, what I want you to do is go to the kitchen and bring me the extra-long wooden spoon that Mrs. Chambers sometimes stirs the soup with, the one with the narrow bowl and the chip in the handle. Can you nudge it back here with your paws?" Clearly the effects of the courage potion hadn't completely worn off, because, without hesitating, Mary scurried onto the floor and disappeared between the bars of the cell.

No one said much while they waited for Mary to return, but an air of quiet hope had filled the dungeon. Dame Bessie stirred and sat up, studying Della with a look of respect. She gave a slow approving nod, as if she could sense what Della was planning.

"You taught me well, Dame Bessie," Della said, praying that her plan would work. But as time wore on, she began to worry, imagining Mrs. Chambers swatting Mary with the broom or tossing her outside by the tail—not an unusual practice in the kitchen.

"Is she coming back?" Gwyneth asked after what felt like an extremely long time.

"Yes, of course she is," Della said, staring at the bars and willing Mary to appear. When the furry rat finally scuttled into view, pushing along a wooden spoon with its nose, Gwyneth clapped, and Della broke into a huge smile.

"So what do you need a spoon for?" Faye asked. "I don't understand."

"To escape," Della said, walking over to the bars and peering through them. It was dark and cold, and water dripped from the ceiling, but there were no guards in sight. Clearly, they didn't like being down here any more than the witches did. "This is a beech spoon," Della whispered. "It works almost as well as a wand. So I'm going to turn us into rats and get us out of here." There was an excited gasp from the girls, followed by an explosion of chatter. "Shhh, we have to keep our voices down." Della crouched beside Mary. "Now you, Mary, have to do something even more courageous." Mary's pale blue eyes were fixed right on Della as if she were listening intently. "I want you to go to Ivan's room. It's on the main upstairs corridor beside Lord and Lady Hepworth's. Go inside and change back into Mary. Once you've done that, you can't become a rat again, because you don't have a wand, so you're going to need to be careful." Mary nodded, and Della continued. "Tell Ivan we don't have much time," Della stressed, "and his uncle really is on his way to attack the castle. Tell him to meet us outside behind the stables and to bring something made from each of our woods. So, Faye is hawthorn; Isolda and Gwyneth are oak. Willow is apple."

"And I'm beech," Dame Bessie said, sounding more like herself.

"Why do we need Ivan's help?" Faye questioned. "Once we're out of here, why not take a boat to the land you come from, Della, and never step foot in this place again?"

"No." Della shook her head and swiped a hand across her face, trying to keep her emotions in check. "We can't run away. We have an army to stop." She looked around at the girls. "If we manage to do it, that will show Lord Hepworth we're not evil."

"Della is right," Dame Bessie agreed.

"But what if Ivan won't help us and tells his father?" Faye said.

"That's what I was thinking," Willow whispered, and Isolda gave a worried nod of agreement.

"He'll help," Della answered. And then, as if she was the one who needed convincing: "He's my friend, and he knows me."

After Mary had scampered off, Della faced the others, holding the wooden spoon. She would be in so much trouble if this were Ruthersfield, turning girls into rats. "I'm sorry, Ms. Cray, but I have no choice," Della said softly, pointing the spoon at Faye. "This shouldn't hurt, Faye."

"Just do it," Faye said. "Get it over with, please."

"Wait for me and I'll lead the way," Della instructed. "We need to stay together, and I know the castle." She took a deep breath and waved the spoon as if it were a wand. "Mutatiarno rat!" Della uttered. A cloud of red smoke exploded from the handle end, and where Faye had been standing, an extremely plump rat with a spoon-shaped tail now sat.

"It looks funny," Gwyneth said.

"The spoon must have distorted the magic a little bit. But it's adorable," Della cooed. "So cute and cuddly. All plump and furry and—" The rat bared its teeth at Della, and she realized she was getting off topic. "And so long as it can get through the bars, that's okay. I don't think anyone will notice."

"Me next," Willow said, scrunching up her eyes, and one after the other Della turned the rest of the girls into rats, all with the same spoon-shaped tails.

"You're not leaving me behind," Dame Bessie said as Della stood in front of her, hesitating.

"It just seems so disrespectful, Dame Bessie."

"I've never heard such nonsense. This is about survival, Della. You know that. And it's better that than leaving me here to rot."

"Okay then," Della agreed, pointing the spoon at Dame Bessie. "Mutatiarno rat."

Not wasting a second now in case they were discovered, Della tapped her left leg, and whispered the transformation spell, changing herself into a plump, furry rat. Immediately she was bombarded by smells, the damp of the dungeon and the smoky ashy scent of the kitchen from up above. Della's nose trembled, and she had a sudden urge to hunt out the tangy bit of goat cheese she was sure she could smell. Her brain went all fuzzy, and for a moment she forgot what she was meant to be doing, scurrying around the room, sniffing at a fossilized bread crumb. It was only when she bumped her tail against the wall that Della remembered. The pain cleared her head, and making sure the other rats were following, Della squeezed through the bars and darted off along the stone corridor. It led upward toward the kitchen, and before Della could scamper underneath the door, Tom Foolery pushed it open, coming the other way. Della couldn't see his face, but he seemed to be in a great hurry, and she squeaked in distress as one of his pointed shoes almost crushed her. He had to be going to check on them, Della thought in a panic, because the only place that corridor led was to the dungeons. Her rat ears quivered, and she could hear him muttering something about witches under his breath. Knowing it wouldn't be long before he sounded the alarm, Della sped up, leading the rats past him and across the kitchen floor, straight by Mrs. Chambers. She stood at the table, yawning and slicing bread, while the kitchen staff shuffled about, rubbing sleep from their eyes.

"I can't believe it. I really can't," Mrs. Chambers said, talking to Myrtle, who was crouched in front of the hearth, using a pair of bellows to get the fire going. "To think little Della is a witch. Honestly, it gives me the chills, remembering how close we were to her."

"You'd never know it," Myrtle agreed as Mrs. Chambers suddenly shrieked and leaped away from the table.

"What in heavens is the matter?" Myrtle said.

"Someone disturbed a rat's nest," Mrs. Chambers

screeched, grabbing a broom and swiping at Della. "Open the door, Myrtle. Quickly now." The rats ran faster, but it was difficult to move swiftly with a spoon-shaped tail and an angry Mrs. Chambers trying to bash you.

Della scurried outside, shocked at how different the world looked when you were only a few inches from the ground. It was difficult to see much, but her nose led the way, following the musky tang of horses toward the stables. She skidded around the corner, claws scrabbling in the dirt, her tail banging against the stone wall. The rest of the witches followed, running in circles and sniffing at the ground as they waited for Della to turn them back. The problem, Della realized, after she had changed herself into a girl again, was that performing a transformation hex on someone else required a separate reversal spell to turn them back. Which Della couldn't perform, because her spoon was still in the dungeon.

"I'm very sorry," Della whispered, kneeling down in front of the rats. "We're going to have to wait for Ivan. I just need a bit of beech wood," she added, "and I'll have you all back to normal in no time."

The rats scowled at Della, their furry brows creasing, and their eyes going all squinty. And one of them (Della wasn't sure who, but she had a strong suspicion it was Faye) scampered up and nipped her on the leg.

Chapter Twenty-Two

....

An Unusual Way to Fly

I'M SURE IT WON'T BE LONG," DELLA KEPT SAYING AS they waited for Ivan to show up. She tried not to think about all the things that might have happened. What if Mary had got knocked on the head with a broom before she had time to change back? Or she might have forgotten how to turn herself into a girl again and still be running around the castle as a rat. Or (and this didn't bear thinking about) what if Ivan didn't want to help them? "Oh, please stop squeaking," Della begged the rats, sensing their crankiness.

There was also the worry that Tom Foolery was, right this very minute, gathering a search party together to find them. At least the rats would be able to hide. She was a sitting target, and Della crouched on the ground, pressed up against the wall. "Ivan," she whispered. "Where are you?"

Della could hear footsteps crunching across the yard, a stable hand whistling, and the creak of the well handle being turned. Soon the castle would be alive with people, knights and guests milling about, getting ready for the big jousting competition. The knot in Della's stomach got tighter and tighter until she could barely breathe. Her eyes ached from straining to see Ivan, and when he finally staggered round the corner, his arms full, Della thought she might faint from relief. Especially because there was Mary, hurrying after him carrying a little stool.

"You came!" Della cried out, forgetting to whisper.

Ivan dropped the pile of wooden things he was carrying on the ground. "Of course I came. I may not like jousting, but I'm still a knight, and you don't leave a damsel in distress."

"Even if that damsel is a witch?"

"I'm not my father, Della. I don't have to think like he does. And if my uncle really is on his way to attack the castle, we've got to stop him."

"Oh, Ivan. This probably isn't very ladylike, but I don't care," Della said, giving him a hug. Letting go, she turned and squeezed Mary. "Well done, Mary. You're the best."

"I think those rats are trying to tell you something," Mary whispered.

The rats were running around Della, nipping at her heels. "Gosh, I'm sorry. Yes they are. I need beech wood, Ivan, quickly."

"Here's a spoon and a broom," Ivan said, poking through the heap. He held them out, and Della took the spoon. It was longer and sturdier than the one she had used before, but Della could feel the flow of energy as she held it.

"Perfect," she whispered. "Now I just need to remember the reversal spell Dame Bessie taught us." A sharp nip on the ankle told her to get on with it. The spell was a slight variation on the one listed in the "Emergency Action" section at the back of *Advanced Magic*, one of the Ruthersfield school textbooks. Not that the girls were ever, under any circumstances, allowed to practice those spells, but Della had flicked through them for fun.

"Ficklebackelroo," she called out softly, waving the spoon at the rats. There was a huge cloud of pink smoke, much bigger than usual, and Della watched in horror as it drifted up over the stables, little sparks of silver shooting out. "Grab your woods," Della cried in a panic, sitting astride the spoon. "Help them, Ivan." She pointed at Willow. "She's an apple, and Faye right there is hawthorn—"

"That was not pleasant," Willow grumbled, her nose still twitching as she stumbled around in a daze. She took the enormous mixing bowl Ivan handed her and peered inside. "What do I do with this?"

"Fly on it," Della ordered, nodding at Mary, who had settled herself on the pear wood stool.

Faye looked totally bemused as Ivan shoved a lute into her hands. "I can't fly on this," she complained, holding up the instrument.

"You have no choice," Della said, suddenly freezing. Even though the tinkling of bells announced his arrival, she still gave a muffled shriek as Tom Foolery leaped around the corner.

"You traitor," Della fumed, taking in the jester's wild eyes. "You're a thief and a traitor."

Tom Foolery stepped closer, and Della gasped in terror, certain he was about to grab her.

"Hurry," the jester panted. "The guards are coming." Della stared at him in confusion. "Go. Now," Tom Foolery mouthed, jumping back out into the yard and jangling his bells. "Good morning, good morning to everyone, and a fine, bright day it is too."

"Out of our way, foolish jester," Della heard one of

the guards bark, followed by the sound of scuffling as they shoved Tom Foolery aside.

There was no time to question why the jester should be trying to help them, and Della certainly wasn't going to hang around to find out. Crouching over the spoon, she gripped the wooden handle, hoping that if she could fly on a beech branch, she could fly on this. "Avante," Della said, and with a surprisingly powerful lurch the spoon rose into the air.

"Avante," Mary cried, wobbling off the ground on her stool. "It works, Della! I'm flying."

"Me too!" Willow shrieked, swooping after Mary in the wooden bowl. Isolda sat on a jousting pole that almost took Della's eye out as she zoomed past, and Faye had somehow managed to perch on the hawthorn lute, which was playing an airy melody as it flew. Bobbing along behind them came little Gwyneth, riding a big oak ladle.

Glancing over her shoulder, Della saw Dame Bessie struggling to take off on a broom. One of the knights had grabbed the other end and was trying to pull it out of her hands.

"I refuse to surrender!" Dame Bessie cried, clearly back to her old vigor. Not hesitating, Della spun her spoon around, and using the handle end like a wand, she aimed it at the knight. Shouting out the transformation spell, Della changed him into a hare.

"Nicely done," Dame Bessie gasped, soaring away. "Oh, this handles very well. We should all be flying on brooms."

"They're chasing after us!" Willow cried, holding on to the sides of the bowl and peering down. "On horseback."

"I wish I didn't have to keep doing this," Della panted. "Keep flying toward the river. I'll catch up," she instructed the others.

"I'm right behind you, Della," Dame Bessie called out, and diving down, the two witches ducked a flurry of speeding arrows.

"We're trying to help you," Della yelled, "but you don't leave us much choice." Hovering in the air, she pointed the end of her spoon at the knights. Dame Bessie joined her, and together they sent a whoosh of magic straight at Lord Hepworth's army. This was what gave witches a bad name, Della thought, as the men changed into a mess of long-legged, fluffy-tailed hares, and the horses started munching on grass. Dame Bessie gave a loud whoop of triumph that really didn't help their image, and trying not to think what Ms. Cray would say, Della turned to speed back toward the others.

Chapter Twenty-Three

....

Crystal Balls Don't Lie

WHAT AM I DOING? DELLA WONDERED, FLYING HIGHER and faster than she knew was safe, especially on a wooden spoon. What had happened to not interfering with the past? Because not only was she interfering, she was probably changing the entire course of history, and who knew what that might mean for the future. But she couldn't stand by and do nothing, waiting for them all to be burned along with Castle Hepworth. Della could see the strange band of witches up ahead, accompanied by faint strains of lute music.

"Tell me your plan," Dame Bessie called out, her

long hair streaming behind her. "When we find Lord Hepworth's brother?"

"I don't quite know yet," Della panted, not having thought that far ahead. She'd been too busy escaping to work out what would happen next, although now that they were airborne, this seemed like rather poor planning. Defeating an army wasn't the sort of magic they had learned at Ruthersfield, so she was definitely going to need Dame Bessie's help.

"We could send the land rolling back like a great rug and trap the scoundrels inside," Dame Bessie said. "Or stir up a wind and blow them right across the waters to Spain?" She reached out a hand and steadied Gwyneth as the little girl hit a wind pocket, almost slipping off the ladle. "There's also a nice shrinking spell, which would make them no taller than my little finger," Dame Bessie continued rather breathlessly. "We could put them in a box and give them to Master Ivan to play with."

"Shrinking seems a bit wicked," Della gasped out, "but the rug idea is good." She caught her breath for a moment, looking down at the River Ribble. It was a cold, bright morning, and the surface of the water ruffled like dark velvet. There was so much land stretching in all directions that Della couldn't help feeling a little sorry for Lord Hepworth's brother, being left a pig farm in the wilds of Scotland while Lord Hepworth got all of this.

Gwyneth gave a bubble of laughter, smiling at a bird flapping past. Her curls whipped around her face as she held on to the ladle, and Della wondered how anyone could think she was evil.

"Oh, look," Willow suddenly exclaimed, bobbing along in the bowl. "Down there. On the other side of that hill." Della followed Willow's gaze toward a camp that had been tucked away from view. There were horses milling about and a few tattered-looking tents. It was the picture she had seen in the crystal ball.

"Stay high," Della ordered in alarm. "We can't be seen."

But it was too late. A guard they hadn't noticed standing on the hill suddenly blew a horn. He was pointing in their direction, and the camp quickly stirred into action.

Della could hear the cry of "Witches!" echoing off the hills, and Gwyneth started to cry.

"Keep calm, Gwyn, it's okay," Della said, worried that she might fall off.

Gwyneth nodded as the cries came again. "Witches!"

A shower of flaming arrows shot toward them, and even though they were flying too high to get hit, Della still swerved. "I'm getting really tired of being used as target practice," she panted.

"To the woods," Dame Bessie ordered. "Now."

• • •

The girls huddled in a thicket of trees. Dame Bessie had drawn an invisibility circle around them with the end of her broom, which meant that they couldn't be seen so long as they stayed inside, but it also meant they ran the risk of being bumped into. The invisibility circle couldn't make them vanish, just hide them from view, so they stood close together, hoping some big-booted knight wouldn't kick them accidently and realize they were there. Della's whole body ached (from being scrunched into a rat shape, followed by riding on a wooden spoon), and it was agony not to move while they waited for the knights to give up their search. Three or four times the men marched past the witches and once stopped right beside them, a booted foot inches from the circle. Della could see a big hole in the toe of the boot, and the knight it belonged to also had a rip in his tunic.

"They're not around here," he said. "I have a nose for witches. I can sniff them out from a mile away."

"What do they smell like then?" another knight asked, standing so close to Della she could have reached out and touched his leg.

"Rotten onions and swamp mold."

Mary pressed a hand against her mouth, and Della couldn't tell if she was trying not to laugh or scream, or possibly both.

"They're not here," a gruff-sounding knight muttered, blowing on his chapped hands. "We can report back that we scared them away."

"I can't wait to move into Castle Hepworth," the knight who had made the swamp-mold comment said. "A fire and roast meat for my supper."

"The squire is giving the order to attack on the morrow. We march before dawn. But I don't think we're moving in," the first knight added rather wistfully. "I believe we're burning it down."

After the knights had shuffled off, Dame Bessie whispered, "We'll surprise them tonight, at dusk, just as the light is leaving. They won't be expecting us, but," she added in a somber tone, "it will take all of our magic to cast this enchantment."

Della wasn't sure how well the lute or the bowl would conduct the attack spell. Luckily, the spoons worked very nicely, as did Dame Bessie's broom and the jousting pole. Della had broken one of the legs off Mary's stool, because it was easier for Mary to hold, and they all practiced rolling up a small field, much to the distress of a number of field mice and rabbits.

With each attempt Della felt more and more uneasy. This went against everything she had been taught about magic. But, Della kept reminding herself, she wasn't at the academy anymore. And if she wanted to see Ivan in the future, she had to save Castle Hepworth and show Ivan's father that witches were not the evil, terrible creatures he imagined—even if it meant breaking nearly every rule in the Ruthersfield handbook.

Chapter Twenty-Four

....

How to Defeat an Army

DELLA COULDN'T HELP THINKING ABOUT HER FAMILY as she followed Dame Bessie and the others toward the camp. How her mum never minded when Della used to make camps under the kitchen table, covering the floor with all the cushions from the living room and hanging blankets around the edges for walls. Robbie used to crawl in after her, and they would sit there eating cookies, waiting for Henry and Sam to try to sneak in.

"Careful," Faye whispered as Della tripped over a tree root, stumbling into her. "You're not looking where you're going."

"Sorry," Della apologized, realizing she needed

to concentrate. They walked on in silence for a few moments before Della whispered, "I wonder if Lord Hepworth and his brother ever got along."

"They most certainly did," Dame Bessie replied softly. "I remember them as boys, chasing through the woods and laughing, pelting each other with acorns, but always in fun. Now no more talk." Dame Bessie put a finger up to her lips. "We're getting close."

They had crept around the hill and were hidden behind a cluster of oak trees. Della spied two of the knights on lookout duty, although they were slumped against each other, and both seemed to have their eyes closed. Clearly they weren't expecting an attack, but they didn't look ready to carry out an attack either. The camp was close enough now for Della to see how tired and hungry the men looked. Most of them were sitting around the fire, which seemed to be more of a smoldering fizzle. There was an iron pot in the embers but no steam coming out, so Della guessed it was empty. Some of the men chewed on what looked like hard crusts of bread, while others simply stared into the distance. Many of the knights had holes in their boots with bits of cloth wrapped around them.

It was easy to pick out Lord Hepworth's brother,

James, pacing around the fire, sweeping his arm in a wide circle. Della could hear him speaking in a loud, but slightly hoarse voice, obviously trying to perk up his army.

"By tomorrow eve, all this will belong to me, and each of you will be recognized for your loyalty and bravery." A number of the knights kept yawning, as if they hadn't had much sleep in a while. Which they probably hadn't, Della guessed.

Dame Bessie nodded at the girls and held up her broom. "Are we ready?" she mouthed. Della wasn't sure she was ready at all, but the rest of the girls nodded back. They all raised their makeshift wands in the air, and without really knowing what she was doing, Della jumped in front of them.

"No!" she blurted out softly. "We can't. It's—it's just not what witches do."

"Out of the way, Della," Dame Bessie whispered. "We have to fight them to save ourselves. To get protection from Lord Hepworth."

"Otherwise we're going right back to the dungeon," Faye hissed. At the mention of the word "dungeon," Gwyneth's lip started to wobble.

"I can't." Della shook her head. "Rolling them up is not the answer."

"Then what do you suggest?" Willow snapped, looking into her bowl. "Because I'm tired and hungry, and I want to go home."

Della thought for a minute, a wild idea floating into her head. "Lasagna!" she whispered with a smile. "It's hard to stay mad over lasagna!"

"Lasagna?" Willow looked at the others. "Does anyone know what she's talking about? Because I have no idea."

"I do," Mary said. "And it's wonderful."

"Willow, can I please borrow your bowl?" Della asked. But Willow made no move to hand it over. "Please," Della begged, "it's important."

"This is all I have for protection."

Dame Bessie touched Willow's arm. "Give it to her, Willow," she urged. "I trust that Della knows what she's doing."

Della wasn't at all sure she knew what she was doing, but she had to try. "You mustn't follow me, though," she insisted. "If it goes wrong and I end up getting thrown back in a dungeon, then I'll need you to help me escape."

"You can't go in there alone," Faye whispered. "Not with all those knights. It's far too dangerous."

"Dame Bessie, please?" Della said. "You have to trust me."

"I trust you, but Faye is right." Dame Bessie was silent for a moment, staring into the distance. "Very well," she finally agreed, "but at the first sign of trouble, we're coming in."

Being as quiet as she could manage, Della crept toward a large, freestanding boulder about fifty feet away from the camp. Since she was approaching from the trees, it was easy to slip in unnoticed. Della crouched behind the stone, trying not to think that this was a completely mad idea. She ran her fingers through her hair, tugging at the knots. The fact that she couldn't remember when she had last washed it was not a good sign, and if she wanted Lord Hepworth's brother to take her seriously, then she couldn't go strolling in with wild witchy hair. Waving the spoon above her, Della said a quick tidy up spell, happy to discover she had a head full of neatly woven braids again.

"All right, here goes," Della murmured, and brandishing the spoon over the bowl, she whispered, "Italiomama." Almost immediately a delicious aroma of bubbling cheese filled the air, and Della could see men lifting up their heads to sniff.

"Anybody hungry?" Della called out, carrying the bowl into the camp and hoping that the men wouldn't recognize her as one of the wild-haired witches from earlier.

"State your name," a knight barked, scrambling to his feet and marching over.

"I'm Della Dupree of Potts Bottom. And I thought I'd make you something to eat." Just the smell of the lasagna gave her confidence, and Della held her head high as she walked toward them, trying to take deep, slow breaths, although she could feel her heart racing.

James Hepworth eyed her suspiciously. "If you come from Potts Bottom, you've been sent by my brother, and this is bound to be poisoned."

"I can assure you it isn't," Della said, sticking her spoon in to take a taste. She flapped a hand in front of her mouth and hopped about. "Hot, hot—but delicious."

"Why would you do such a thing?" James asked, and Della couldn't help noticing that he had a big holey run in his woolly tights.

"I've been watching you," Della admitted. "And you all look rather cold and extremely hungry."

"We are," one of the knights said, ignoring his leader's scowl. "Well, we are. Very." He held out a hard crust of bread, and Della covered it with the gooey, bubbling lasagna.

"This should warm you up."

"Very well, you may test it for us," James said, not that the knight needed permission. He had already lifted the crust up to his face and inhaled deeply. Della watched him pick off a crispy edge piece of lasagna and pop it into his mouth. A look of such ecstasy rolled across his eyes that James asked, "How is it?"

"Like heaven in my mouth," the knight replied.

And without hesitating, the rest of the knights gathered around the bowl, using their fingers and bits of stick to scoop up the lasagna. They ate and ate until their bellies were full and drops of sauce and cheese clung to their beards.

"The most wondrous meal of my life," one of the knights sighed, licking his greasy fingers.

"Now let's get a fire going and warm you all up," Della suggested, knowing that this was the risky part, using magic in front of them. Actually, it wasn't just risky; it was extremely dangerous and probably very stupid. But the knights were calm and well fed and could (hopefully) see that she didn't want to hurt them. Della waved her spoon over the embers, murmuring a simple fire spell. Within seconds the ashes had burst into life, and a blazing fire drew the men close. Except for a red-haired knight who shielded his face with his hands.

"'Tis sorcery!" he cried out. "Such a thing cannot be done without powers."

"Then she must be an angel," a small, bearded knight said in all seriousness, warming himself near the flames.

Della smiled at him. "Show me your boots, please. You can't walk in those. They're coming apart at the seams." The knight stood in front of Della, and she tapped each of his boots with her spoon. "Fixirpiccilo," she chanted, and the leather sewed itself neatly back up.

"See, an angel!" The knight grinned. "Now I can march without getting my feet wet."

"Exactly. Nothing worse than wet feet," Della agreed. She looked around the circle of men. "If you all line up, I can fix everyone's boots."

"Sire, there is witchcraft at work here. Can't you see it?" The red-haired knight paced about, throwing furtive glances at Della. "We are being trapped in a web of kindness."

"Then I like being trapped," one of the knights in front of the fire said, holding out a stale crust. "Can I have more of . . . What did you say it was called?"

"Lasagna," Della said, spooning another helping onto the fossilized chunk of bread.

As each of the men came up, Della fixed their boots and mended any tears in their clothes. "Much better," she said, keeping an eye on Lord Hepworth's brother, who kept glancing her way and was clearly keeping an eye on her, too. Finally, with a perplexed shake of his head, he came over and sat down beside her. The fire burned brightly as the men lolled in front of it, happy and content.

"Why are you doing this?" he asked

Staring into the flames for a minute, Della turned to him and said, "Because I don't think you're a bad person. And it's nice to be able to help."

James gave her a searching look. "Witch or angel, what are you?"

Before Della could reply, the redheaded knight yelled out, "Invaders! Invaders! Attacking from the river!"

At first Della thought it must be Dame Bessie and the others coming to rescue her, until she heard the pounding of hoofs. And even though the light had faded, Della could still make out the bulk of Lord Hepworth, riding into the camp on his horse. Another horse galloped beside him, and hopping along behind, much to Della's dismay, came an army of angry hares.

....

Chapter Twenty-Five

Not So Scary after All

B Y THE LIGHT FROM THE FIRE DELLA COULD SEE LORD Hepworth's normally flushed face glowing an even deeper shade of crimson, whether from the riding or the shock of seeing Della in conversation with his brother, it was hard to tell.

"You, you—traitorous witch," Lord Hepworth spluttered, sliding from his horse and pointing a finger at Della. "Mixing with the enemy."

Ivan jumped down from the second horse. "Father, Della is not a traitor. She warned you about this attack."

"You warned him?" James said, his face clouding with anger.

"And how did she know? Because she's a witch," Lord Hepworth fumed.

"A good witch that makes lasagna and mends our boots," one of the knights murmured, giving a sleepy belch.

"She's still evil," Lord Hepworth stated.

"Della isn't evil," Ivan said stoutly. "You know that, Father, and from the look of things here, you do too, Uncle James."

Lord Hepworth gestured at the hares, which, Della could now see, had ears the same spoon shape as the rats' tails. "Then how do you explain this . . . this monstrous magic?"

The hares had flopped on the ground and appeared to be breathing heavily. One of James's knights suddenly pounced on them, picking up a hare in each hand and swinging them around by the ears. "Hare stew," he cried out.

"Put those down," Lord Hepworth bellowed, scaring the knight into dropping them. "Those hares are not for eating, you numskull."

"Will you all please calm down?" Della said, relieved that Ivan was here. She hoped Dame Bessie was keeping an eye on things, because from the way the brothers were glaring at her, Della had a strong suspicion she was going to need rescuing. "Look, I am not a traitor, or evil or any of the terrible things you think, okay?"

"Turning my knights into hares isn't evil?"

"They were firing arrows and trying to catch us. And I was planning to turn them back again."

"You escaped from my dungeon," Lord Hepworth said, seething.

"But you shouldn't have locked us up in the first place," Della snapped. "We hadn't done anything wrong."

"You're witches!"

"Yes, and that is not a crime," Della exploded, anger taking over from fear.

"Talking to my brother is a big crime," Lord Hepworth said. "Plotting with him to burn down Castle Hepworth."

"I am not plotting anything, and your brother is no more evil than I am."

"He is indeed," Lord Hepworth blustered. "He tried to run a knife through me in my own bed."

"I did not," James interrupted hotly. "That is lies. All lies. Who told you such a thing?"

"My servant saw you creeping up in the night."

"To talk with you, not to run a knife through you. Although I can't pretend I didn't feel like doing it, especially after your servant chased me off. Why do you get everything?" James complained. "The title, the lands, the castle, the villages, and I get a pig farm?"

"It's the law," Lord Hepworth pointed out. "I am the oldest brother."

"By a few moments, that's all," James growled.

"Which does seem a little unfair," Della said, giving Lord Hepworth a meaningful look. "Perhaps you could share with your brother? I mean, you have an awful lot of land and a great many villages, don't you?"

The brothers eyed each other sourly. "You really weren't trying to kill me?" Lord Hepworth muttered.

"No. But I was planning to attack the castle," James admitted. "It's hard to be so far away from where we grew up and to see you with everything. You had no right to banish me."

Lord Hepworth sighed. "You were banished because I thought you wanted to hurt me. And all that stomping about the castle and yelling. Your behavior was disgraceful."

"But if you had been the younger twin, you would probably have behaved disgracefully too," Della pointed out.

"I might," Lord Hepworth agreed rather grudgingly.

"So now that we've cleared that up, how about you both shake hands and be friends again. No more talk of running knives through each other or burning down castles, okay?" Della could hear them both grumbling to themselves, and she went on. "Remember how much fun you used to have playing in the woods when you were boys? Chasing each other and having acorn fights?"

There was a rather long silence, and then Lord Hepworth said, "How about if I give you Potts Bottom? You can build yourself a nice house and live comfortably with the rents from the village. There's plenty of land for your knights, too."

James pondered this for a moment and then gave a firm nod. "Very well, brother. That sounds fair enough." And as Della and Ivan watched, something truly miraculous happened. The brothers grinned at each other and awkwardly hugged.

Ivan raised his eyebrows. "I never thought I'd see that happen," he murmured.

"My mum always tells my brothers that talking it out is much better than fighting," Della said. And wanting to keep the peace going, she decided that this was a good time to turn the hares back into knights. Della waved her spoon at them, watching the magic flow out in an explosion of turquoise smoke. Her arm tingled, and she gave a yelp. This sort of powerful magic really needed a proper wand. The knights went tumbling about like puppies. They untangled themselves and stood up, looking dazed and slightly confused.

"I'm famished," one of them said. "All that hopping is exhausting."

"Make them some lasagna," James suggested, and there was a great cry of agreement at this.

So Della whipped up a fresh pot, which Lord Hepworth declared even more delicious than pheasant stew.

"I had no idea magic could taste this good," he said, licking tomato sauce out of his beard.

"Because you don't understand it, that's why. Where I come from, magic is a wonderful thing. We like to use it to help people and fix things. Witches are respected, not locked up in dungeons."

"Look at our boots," James said, showing off the repairs Della had made.

"And Della healed a really nasty cut on my leg," Ivan added.

"Yes, and why do you think your castle has been so tidy lately and smelled so good?" Della questioned. "That's all magic, Lord Hepworth."

"But our witches are not like yours," Lord Hepworth said, beginning to sound unsure. "They put hexes on people and turn milk sour, flying about on pigs and scaring villagers."

Della shook her head in frustration. "It's because they haven't been taught how to use their magic properly, so it leaks out in dangerous ways." Turning toward the woods, she beckoned and shouted, "Dame Bessie? Dame Bessie, come here."

"What is this? What's going on?" Lord Hepworth spun his head back and forth as Dame Bessie and the others walked toward them, Faye carrying Gwyneth, and Willow holding Isolda and Mary by the hands.

"These girls are all witches," Della said, causing Lord Hepworth to take a step back. He glanced over at his guards, his hand hovering close to his sword. "Don't look so scared. They're not going to hurt you," Della continued, but Lord Hepworth didn't seem convinced. "This is the problem," Della snapped, realizing that she was actually standing up to Lord Hepworth. These words were definitely coming out of her mouth, not just floating around in her head. And she suddenly wished that Anna and Sophie could hear her, defending witches like this. But Anna and Sophie weren't here, and Della stopped for a moment, taking a shaky breath. She couldn't think about her friends right now. "Just because you and the rest of the country don't understand about witches, they have to live in fear of getting caught," she finished up. Both brothers and all the knights were staring at Dame Bessie and the girls, who looked, Della thought, about as dangerous as a gaggle of kittens. As the silence stretched on, Gwyneth gave a little hop and a wave, calling over, "Witches are vewwy nice."

"But this is ridiculous," James finally burst out. "These girls need protecting, not persecuting."

"And that's just what Dame Bessie's been doing," Della said. "Teaching us how to survive so we don't get caught. Except it's dangerous magic," Della added. "Not the sort of stuff witches should be learning. No one wants to go around turning knights into hares, but you don't give us much choice."

"Well." Lord Hepworth hung his head for a moment. "Well," he said again. "I had no idea."

"We should be teaching them to make lasagna and mend boots," James pointed out.

"Exactly," Della agreed, giving Lord Hepworth's brother her warmest smile. "Finally, someone who gets it."

"So let's start a school for witches," James suggested, enjoying being the popular brother. "A place where they can learn all these useful things."

"Wait!" Della panicked, suddenly realizing what James was proposing. "It's too soon." She looked around in alarm. "This isn't how it happens."

"I'll give you a nice piece of land in Potts Bottom," James said generously. "You can build your school there."

"That's my land," Lord Hepworth said.

"No, you just gave it to me, remember?"

"You did, Father," Ivan reminded him, and then

under his breath, "Let's not start another fight."

"And what shall we call it?" James said. "The school needs a name."

"Dupree Academy?" Ivan suggested. "After you, Della."

"*No*, you can't call it that. It's not the right name at all." This was all going terribly wrong. Who knew what would happen in the future if Ruthersfield were called Dupree?

"Well, since you've been teaching these girls already," Lord Hepworth said, turning to Dame Bessie, "perhaps we should call it after you?"

"Bessie Academy." Mary giggled. "That sounds funny!"

"What is your full name, mam?" Lord Hepworth inquired.

"Oh, I'm too old for such nonsense as this," Dame Bessie muttered.

"No you're not," Faye insisted. "Come on, Dame Bessie."

"Very well." And Dame Bessie actually blushed. "It's Dame Elizabeth Ruthersfield."

Della's mouth dropped open. She let out a soft gasp, and Ivan grabbed her as she started to sway.

"Are you all right?" Ivan said. "You look like you've seen a ghost."

"I think—I mean—" Della stammered, feeling too hot then too cold as she tried to sort out what she did mean.

"Do you want to sit down?" Ivan suggested.

"I can't believe this," Della murmured, giving a slightly hysterical laugh.

"Believe what?" Ivan said, and Della could see him looking at her as if she'd gone mad.

"I'm Witch Dupree," Della whispered, trying to absorb what she had just figured out. "There isn't another one with red hair and pots of courage who's off fighting dragons, Ivan! I mean, I am Witch Dupree!" Della shook her head in amazement. "I thought I'd messed everything up, but this is how it happens. This is the start of Ruthersfield."

"So you approve of the name?" Lord Hepworth asked. "Because without you there wouldn't be a witch school."

"Of course I approve," Della said, laughing harder.

"Ruthersfield Academy!" Lord Hepworth nodded. "I like that. It will be the first official school for magic in the country."

"In Potts Bottom," James reminded him.

"You can help teach," Dame Bessie suggested. "You'll be a wonderful teacher, Della."

"Wait, no." Della felt as if she'd just been dunked in a bucket of cold water. Her laughter dried up as she stared at Dame Bessie. "I don't want to teach."

"You don't?" Lord Hepworth inquired.

"I'm not meant to be a teacher." Della swallowed around the lump in her throat. "I want to go home," she said softly, her voice cracking. But this was her home now. And there was no point in waiting for Witch Dupree to turn up and sort everything out, because (although it didn't seem nearly so funny anymore) she clearly wasn't coming.

Chapter Twenty-Six

....

Courage

EARLY THE NEXT MORNING LORD HEPWORTH AND HIS brother returned to the castle accompanied by a great many knights and a group of exhausted witches. At the sound of horses' hooves, Lady Hepworth, their guests, and the rest of the castle staff rushed into the courtyard, astonished to see the brothers riding over the drawbridge together, and even more amazed to witness a number of knights and witches chattering away, as if they were all coming back from a fun day out and not a battlefield. Tom Foolery stood at the edge of the gathering, fidgeting and ringing his bells, more from nervousness than any feelings of joy, Della sensed. Why had he turned them in and then tried to help them escape? It didn't make sense. She caught the jester's eye, and he immediately performed a series of handsprings across the cobblestones, impressing the crowd, but leaving Della with the distinct feeling that he was once again trying to avoid her as he disappeared inside the castle.

"Don't look so sad, Della," Dame Bessie murmured, pulling her aside. "You can't stay away from home forever. Not because of a lost necklace."

"I'm not sure anymore that Tom Foolery has it," Della said, aware that in all the commotion she hadn't mentioned her biggest worry to Dame Bessie.

"Then you must be brave and tell your parents. I'm sure they will understand."

"It's not that simple," Della said, wondering how to begin, wondering if Dame Bessie might actually know something about time travel. Lowering her voice, Della whispered, "What if I told you I came from another time, as well as another place? Could you help me get back there?"

"I'm not sure I understand. Are you talking about the future?"

Della nodded. "Can you time-travel, Dame Bessie?" Just saying the words gave her a shiver of hope. "Is there anything in the grimoire that tells you how to move through time?"

Dame Bessie looked at Della for a long moment. "Is that what the necklace did?"

"Yes," Della admitted, brushing a sleeve across her face. "And now I'm stuck here. But you can help me, can't you? You have to be able to."

"I wish I could," Dame Bessie said softly, touching Della's arm. "But I'm afraid that is an impossible sort of magic."

"It's not impossible," Della sighed. "It just doesn't get invented until the fifteenth century."

Lord Hepworth had suggested a banquet in Della's honor, for helping bring about peace between the brothers, and for showing him the joys of magic. He ordered the portrait of Lord James to be dusted off and hung alongside his own splendid painting. "And everyone is invited," he announced, indicating Dame Bessie and the rest of the witches, who were gathered in the great hall. "Bring your families, and we will all celebrate." At the mention of "families," Della's stomach clenched, but she tried to be happy for the others.

Since none of the girls felt too keen about returning to their villages alone, with the mark of a witch hanging over them, Lord Hepworth sent along a contingent of knights to offer protection and explain what had happened.

"I'm not sure what my family will say," Mary said anxiously. "I'm quite certain they still hate witches."

"It's going to take a long time to change how people feel," Della told her, "but a school is a good place to start. You're going to love Ruthersfield, Mary. I promise."

"You sound as if you know what it's like."

"I can imagine," Della said with a sigh. "We have witch schools where I come from, and I really liked mine."

Dame Bessie took Della's hand and squeezed it. "And it will be wonderful to have your help in setting this one up."

"Ladies," Lord Hepworth called out, striding over to them. "I was thinking about a coat of arms and a school motto, like the grand universities have."

"Perhaps *Praticus ladamay*?" Dame Bessie suggested, glancing at Della.

"What does that mean?" Della asked. "I've never heard it before."

"Protect yourself," Dame Bessie said, and then, noting Della's reaction: "You don't look too sure?"

"Well, it's not about teaching girls how to survive anymore. It's about teaching them to love magic. To be good witches," Della reminded her.

"How about *Kibet fallow da*? That was something the first high priestess of magic wrote about. It means to follow your passion." Dame Bessie turned to Lord Hepworth and added rather frostily, "Because let's not forget there was a time when witches followed their passion quite openly."

"I like that," Lord Hepworth said. "'Follow your passion' it is! And our coat of arms shall be a cauldron for cooking lasagna in."

Della couldn't help thinking how strange and dreamlike this all felt. Listening to Dame Bessie come up with the school motto. Being right here for the start of Ruthersfield Academy and still trying to absorb the fact that she was Witch Dupree.

"Are you sure you're feeling all right, Della?" Lord Hepworth inquired. "You don't seem quite yourself."

"I have an excellent reviving tonic I can make you," Dame Bessie murmured. "In case you are in need of it."

"I do feel very tired," Della said, wondering if a reviving tonic could stop her heart from aching.

"Not surprising after all that has happened," Dame Bessie said. "But think how wonderful it will be not to have to hide anymore. To practice witchcraft openly and in a safe place. Honestly, I never thought I'd see this day."

"Nor did I," Della answered truthfully, trying her hardest to see the wonderful.

• • •

The castle bustled with activity, although Tom Foolery was clearly keeping out of sight. There was no time to worry about this now, because Lord Hepworth had asked her to show off a cobweb-sweeping spell to his guests. So Della was demonstrating with one of the castle brooms, making it fly around the great hall by itself, dusting all the cobwebs off the beams. The guests oohed and aahed in fascination, but none of them stood too close to Della, flinching every time she raised her hand.

"And just wait till you try her special stew," Lord Hepworth said. "It's made with a pinch of magic and is magnificently delicious." He beamed at Della proudly. "The girls are going to learn all these spells at Ruthersfield Academy."

"So long as they don't poison us first," someone in the crowd muttered.

"Well, I never thought I'd say this," a lady in a green velvet gown announced, "but there is a small part of me that rather wishes my daughter was a witch."

"Rosanna, no!" another woman said, clapping a hand over her mouth. "Never say such a thing!"

"I'll put up with this as long as you're sure they aren't going to turn evil on us, Hepworth," a lumpish man with a ponytail said. "Start changing us all into pigs." The man snorted and scratched his stomach, and

Della could tell that attitudes weren't going to change overnight.

She looked around for Ivan, needing to see her friend, but he wasn't anywhere in sight. Della guessed he must be outside, getting ready for the big jousting competition that was going to take place after lunch. All the knights were strutting about, trying to outdo each other with chivalrous acts toward the ladies. One of them had even scaled the castle wall to try to rescue a maiden from the north tower, except there wasn't a maiden up there to be saved, so he had to come down again, looking rather foolish. They clanked about in their chain mail and big boots, and Della suddenly hoped that Ivan had taken his courage potion. He was going to need all the courage he could get against this lot.

She was just about to head into the kitchen to help Mrs. Chambers whip up a batch of chicken curry when the castle door opened, and in strode Ivan.

"Ahhh, there's my boy," Lord Hepworth bellowed. He turned to his brother. "Now you can see your nephew bring some pride and glory on the Hepworth name."

Ivan marched right up to his father and said in a loud, clear voice, "I'm not going to be entering the competition, Father."

"Excuse me?" Lord Hepworth said, wiggling a finger

around in his ear. "I don't think I heard you properly."

"I don't want to joust. I don't like jousting, and I'm tired of pretending I do." Ivan reached into his tunic pocket and took out a little wooden carving of a figure sitting on a horse. The figure was holding a jousting pole and even wore a helmet. "This is for you."

Lord Hepworth turned it around. "You made this?"

"I carve a lot of things. It's what I like to do."

The guests had grown quiet. "But you're my son," Lord Hepworth blustered. "My only son." His cheeks were turning a rather worrying mottled purple.

"But isn't it wonderful," Della said as everyone turned to look at her. Ignoring the sweat pooling under her arms and the heat in her face, she took a deep breath and continued. "He's following his passion. Just like the motto for Ruthersfield. You should be proud of Ivan, Lord Hepworth. He's got a real talent for carving."

The great hall was silent as Lord Hepworth studied his son. "Maybe you'll change your mind, Ivan?"

"I won't, Father."

"Well, I'm certainly not happy about this."

"But I am," Lady Hepworth said softly, joining the group with a smile. Della saw her pull her shoulders back and stand a little taller as she faced her husband.

"Can I joust in his place?" James suggested. "Some-one needs to hold up the family honor."

Lord Hepworth was quiet for a moment, and then he slung an arm around James's shoulder. "Yes indeed, brother. And you must wear the Hepworth colors."

"He wasn't as angry as I expected," Ivan said, talking to Della in the hallway. "Not that he jumped for joy, but he didn't disown me, or send me to my uncle's pig farm."

"I'm sure he'll come around. And that was very brave of you, Ivan, going up to him like that." Della started to giggle. "You drank the courage potion, didn't you! It was meant to give you courage for the jousting competition, not for taking on your father."

"But I didn't drink it," Ivan confessed. "I was going to, but then I thought about how brave you have to be every day, just for being a witch. So I decided to be brave too. And I can't take courage potion every time I feel scared, otherwise I'd always be drinking it."

"Oh, I'm not brave," Della scoffed, but she had to admit she would never have spoken to Lord Hepworth the way she did when she'd first gotten here. "Well, maybe a little bit," she admitted.

A faint jingle of bells came from the far end of the corridor, and Della grabbed Ivan's arm. "Do you hear that?" she said as the jester appeared at the top of the hallway.

Chapter Twenty-Seven

....

How It Began . . .

"MIGHT I SPEAK WITH MISTRESS DELLA ALONE?" TOM
Foolery said, walking up to them without his usual
spring. Della could hear the shakiness in his voice.

"You've been avoiding me," she said.

"I have," the jester admitted, hanging his head. He
cupped his hands together, blew into them, and pulled
out a red silk handkerchief, which he dabbed his eyes
with.

"It's okay, Ivan," Della reassured her friend. "I'm
sure this won't take long. Can you check on Dame Bessie and the others for me? Make sure they're all right,
especially Mary?"

The jester led Della upstairs to his chambers. He didn't say anything until they were safely inside. Scuffling his shoes, Tom Foolery murmured, "I owe you a sincere apology."

"Why did you do it?" Della asked, her anger slipping away, because the jester looked so sorry.

Tom Foolery walked over to the cupboard and took out the crystal ball. "This belonged to my grandmother," he said, rubbing the surface gently. He raised his gaze to meet Della's. "She was a witch too," he confessed. "A good one."

"Your grandmother?"

"She kept it secret, of course, but I would see her call for the rain in a dry season and keep the storms from coming until after the wheat was cut."

"Then you know," Della exploded. "You know witches aren't evil." She couldn't believe what she was hearing. "So why? Why did you turn us in?"

Staring at the floor, Tom Foolery said, "I am ashamed to admit I was jealous."

"Jealous? Seriously?"

"I know what real magic can do. And my magic isn't real. It entertains and amuses, but it's nothing more than smoke and mirrors. People laugh at me." He gave a heavy sigh. "When I look into this crystal ball, I see nothing, and there you were, stirring up visions and purple smoke, just like my grandmother used to." He sniffed and blew his nose on the handkerchief. "Envy is a horrible thing. I should throw myself on a sword, but I'm too much of a coward."

"So you did see," Della said softly.

The jester nodded. "I did, and it made me so bitter I acted in haste. Told the guards and had you followed to Dame Bessie's." He gave another deep sigh. "I regretted it right away, but when I went back to let you out of the dungeons, you had gone." A tear ran down his cheek. "I am the one who should be locked up."

"How long have you known?" Della asked, wondering if he had seen her performing magic around the castle.

"I had my suspicions from the beginning. A glimpse of you in your strange clothes and then that burst of purple light, and the faint burnt-honey scent that reminded me of my grandmother's hut. It smelled like my memory of magic."

"And you didn't say anything?"

Tom Foolery shook his head. "Not at first. I wanted to, but I knew how disappointed my grandmother would be if I betrayed a witch. And I wasn't completely sure until I saw you with her crystal ball."

"Wow," Della murmured. "Wow," she said again. "I had no idea."

"You are still upset. I can tell." Tom Foolery waved his arms around Della. "Well, look what I have here," he said, appearing to pull something out of her ear. The jester held his fists out toward Della. "Which one?" Della tapped the left, and Tom Foolery made a sad face. "Empty."

Dellla sighed, not in the mood for his games. "That one then," she said, pointing at the jester's right hand. Tom Foolery uncurled his fingers, and there, snuggled in the palm of his hand, was the travel amulet, the fossilized dragon's eye winking up at her.

"Oh," Della gasped. "Oh, my necklace." She stared at it, not quite believing what her eyes were telling her.

"Well, aren't you going to take it?"

Della could feel a great sob gathering inside her, of relief and happiness, and utter astonishment. Terrified the travel amulet might vanish again, she scooped it up and slipped the chain over her head. "You did take it."

"I did. And if you want to turn me into a toad, I quite understand. Please go ahead. I'm sure I'll be quite happy living in the castle moat."

Della shuddered. "I'm done with transformation spells. No more turning people into hares or rats or toads."

"That is kind of you and more than I deserve."

Not wanting to waste any more time, Della said, "I must go and say good-bye to everyone."

"Of course."

She stopped at the door, hesitating a moment. "You know you're an excellent entertainer, Tom Foolery. Making people laugh is just as important as real magic. And even I couldn't figure out some of your tricks."

"Thank you." Tom Foolery smiled. "I have a feeling we won't meet again, Della Dupree, but safe travels home, wherever you have come from."

Dame Bessie and the girls' families were gathered around the fire in the great hall. Della was happy to see Mary's parents there, even if they did look extremely uncomfortable, as if this was all too much for them. But her brothers hadn't come, clearly needing a little more time to recover after seeing their sister change into a rat. Faye and Willow were flirting with a couple of knights while Isolda and Gwyneth chased a chicken around the room.

"I have to leave now," Della said, hugging them all good-bye.

"Leave?" Dame Bessie questioned, giving Della a knowing look.

"To go home!" Della grinned.

"Don't you want to stay and come to Ruthersfield with us?" Faye asked. She brandished an imaginary wand. "Dame Bessie is going to teach us all kinds of wonderful spells."

"And we're going to have proper flying lessons," Willow said. "On broomsticks!"

"The bristles act nicely as weights," Dame Bessie said. "Much better than tree branches."

"I'm going to miss you," Mary cried, squeezing Della around the waist. "Please don't go."

Gwyneth came charging over and nudged Mary out of the way. She wrapped her arms around Della's legs, covering them with kisses.

Della laughed. "And I'm going to miss you all so much too. But I also miss my family. And now I've got my necklace back, it's time."

Dame Bessie smiled. "That is wonderful news indeed."

"Did Tom Foolery take it?" Mary whispered.

"He gave it back, Mary. That's all that matters."

Della found Ivan in the stables, sitting in a corner of Chestnut's stall. He was whittling a piece of wood and whistling between his teeth.

"I've come to say good-bye."

"So soon?" Ivan scrambled to his feet. Chestnut immediately whinnied and walked over, rubbing his head against her cheek.

"Oh I'll miss you, too," Della whispered, patting the horse's neck.

"You found what you've been looking for?" Ivan said.

Della nodded, not trusting herself to speak. Much as she couldn't wait to get home, she was going to miss Ivan a lot.

"Will I see you again?" Ivan asked, slipping his whittling knife into his pocket.

"I'm not sure. It's a long way to come."

"Perhaps I could visit you?" Ivan said, which made Della smile.

"My country is rather hard to find." She looked away for a moment, noticing a tiny wooden mouse balanced on top of the stall door. "You must keep carving, Ivan. You're so good, and one day your dad will be proud of you."

"I hope so," Ivan said. "I plan to make a table next."

"But probably best to give up the drawing," Della added with a laugh.

"I'm going to miss you, Della Dupree,"

"Me too," Della said, embarrassed to feel her lip trembling. "I like it here, but I need to get home, Ivan."

"Have you told my father?"

"I'm just working up the courage to do that."

"Do you want some of this?" Ivan asked, taking the little bottle Della had given him out of his pocket.

"No thanks. You keep it. Just in case you ever have to fight any battles."

Lord Hepworth was most upset to hear that Della was leaving, although Dame Bessie promised to send some of the girls up every week, so they could practice their magic in the castle.

"Especially that nice lavender-scented spell," Lord Hepworth said.

"And the lasagna," James added, stepping aside as one of the castle musicians strolled past, strumming a tune on his lute.

"You must teach me the lasagna spell before you go," Dame Bessie said. "It's one I've never seen before." Reaching into the folds of her cloak, she pulled out a small, plain book with a brown leather cover. Della watched Dame Bessie open it. She could see the old woman's spiky handwriting across the paper, and a strange sensation rushed over her, as if she had experienced this exact moment before. The lute played on, and a smell of spices and herbs wafted up from the page.

"I . . ." Della stared at the book. "What is that?"

"Just my little book of spells. I've been writing down some of the things you've shown me, Della, but I don't have the lasagna spell in here." Dame Bessie looked puzzled. "What is the matter, dear? You've gone very pale."

"It's *The Book of Spells*," Della said, staring at the brown leather volume. "The one in our library."

"I'm not quite sure what you're talking about, Della."

"As soon as I opened it, I knew I had to come back here, Dame Bessie. Of course, now it all makes sense!" Della laughed, realizing that there must have been a spell on the book, giving her the idea to try to find Witch Dupree, a time-sensitive spell that activated when she opened the pages. "I think I understand what happened."

"Well, that's good, because I'm rather lost."

"May I borrow this for a moment?" Della asked, holding out her hands. "And your wand, too? I need to do one last piece of magic before I go." She held the book carefully, trying to remember the time-release enchantment they had learned in spells and charms class the day she had left. "I knew this had a spell on it; I just didn't realize it was me who put it there!" Seeing Dame Bessie's confusion, Della said, "It's a little hard to explain. Just promise you'll keep this book safe. It has to live in the Ruthersfield library, so make sure they build one, okay. You can't lose it."

"You have my word, Della."

"Now, it was April the ninth," Della murmured, remembering the day she had traveled back in time. "And I'm quite sure of the time, because I'd just looked at the clock in the library before I sat down. Ten forty, although I should probably add on an extra minute to get over to the table," Della said. "So almost eight hundred years from now, on April the ninth, 2020, at ten forty-one, I'm going to open this book up and decide to send myself back to Potts Bottom." She looked at Dame Bessie. "The old Della would never have been brave enough to do this, you see, time-travel by herself. That's why I have to help me get here." And waving the beech wand over the book, Della felt a great rush of magic race through her as she cast the time-release spell.

"Will I see you again?" Dame Bessie asked, taking the book back from Della.

"I don't think so. But there's no need to worry, Dame Bessie. Ruthersfield Academy is going to be a wonderful school, and will be around for hundreds and hundreds of years."

"Sounds as if you're quite sure about that."

"I am," Della said with a smile, holding on to the travel amulet and remembering that she had a history presentation in a few minutes.

Chapter Twenty-Eight

....

Della Dupree!

SPACE AND TIME SPUN AROUND DELLA, SUCKING HER headfirst into a whirlpool of colored energy. She could sense her surroundings spinning faster and faster until, with a forceful push, she was finally released. Feeling dizzy and sick, Della reached for something to grab on to, stumbling sideways into a desk. She held the edges and leaned over, breathing deeply as she waited for the room to stop turning. The smell of varnished desks and lunchtime meat pie triggered a sense of urgency, reminding her where she was, and before she had fully recovered, Della slid off the amulet and reeled over to put it back in the cupboard. Even though she was still disoriented, she knew she couldn't be discovered with the dragon's eye hanging around her neck.

Hurrying toward the door, Della tripped over her gown, realizing she hadn't changed back into her uniform. "And I don't have a wand," Della groaned, remembering that Mary's mother had thrown her school wand onto the fire. She couldn't go out into the hallway dressed like this. It was like coming to school in your pajamas when it wasn't pajama day. Della glanced around the room in case someone had forgotten a wand, left it lying on a desk, but she couldn't see any. Shoving her hands deep down in her pockets, Della felt the tip of the carved sickle moon that Ivan had given her when they first met. She had completely forgotten about it, because it had slipped through a hole at the bottom of the fabric and was caught in a tangle of thread. Tugging it free, Della pulled the moon out, remembering it was made of beech wood. "Wish I'd found you in the dungeon," Della said, turning it over and seeing the tiny acorn Ivan etched on all of his carvings. She waved the sickle moon in the air, murmured a quick reversal spell, and in a puff of purple smoke, changed the medieval gown back into her school uniform.

The door to the hallway was flung open, and Ms. Randal strode in. "Who is doing magic in here?"

"I'm sorry, Ms. Randal," Della said, attempting to smooth her rumpled skirt. "It was an accident."

"Shouldn't you be outside? It's recess. And what on earth have you been doing, Della Dupree? You're a mess." Ms. Randal wrinkled up her nose. "And where is that unpleasant smell coming from?"

Della sniffed, realizing it was her. Not surprising, since she hadn't bathed in almost two weeks. "We're studying the Middle Ages in history," Della said, deciding to be as honest as she could. "I know they used to use different woods instead of wands, and I was practicing with a piece of raw beech. That's what the smell and the smoke are from."

"Good grief!" Ms. Randal's eyes bugged out in horror. "Using wood in its natural form as a conductor of magic can be extremely dangerous, Della. That is why we have wands and rules and don't go traipsing about the forest using tree branches anymore. Honestly." Ms. Randal pursed her lips. "I do think these history projects get a little out of control sometimes. You'll be turning us all into mice next."

Della bit her lip to stop herself from laughing. "Sorry, Ms. Randal."

"I should by all rights put you on cobweb-sweeping duty after school today," Ms. Randal continued. Della groaned. Cobweb-sweeping duty was given out as detention, and it took forever, flying around the school, sweeping the cobwebs from the corners the old-fashioned way, with the girls on their broomsticks. "But I won't this time," Ms. Randal added, giving Della a small smile.

"Oh, thank you so much, Ms. Randal. It won't happen again—I promise," Della said, escaping into the hallway.

"I should hope not. And tuck your shirt in," Ms. Randal called after her. "This is a school for young witches, not the wilds of medieval England."

There were still five minutes before history class, and Della stopped for a moment, leaning against the wall and closing her eyes. She couldn't quite believe she was back here, that no time had passed, and yet days and days had gone by. A distant clatter of footsteps announced that recess was almost over.

"Oh my gosh. What's that smell?" Melanie's voice echoed down the corridor, loud and unpleasant as always. "Is it you, Katrin? Did you eat any of those nasty pickled herrings you're always bringing in for snack?"

Della opened her eyes, hearing the girls laugh. She saw Katrin walking a little in front of the pack, by herself, her head down and her knitted bag slung over her shoulder.

"I think there should be a rule about eating pickled herrings in school," Cassie said. "They smell so disgusting."

"STOP IT!" Della shouted, stepping out in front of them and thinking how satisfying it would be to turn Melanie into a frog.

"Oh good grief." Melanie pressed a hand over her mouth. "It's not Iceland that smells so bad. It's you, Della."

"Why do you have to be so mean?" Della said, staring right at Melanie. "What has Katrin ever done to you?"

There was some nervous fidgeting among the girls, and Melanie flushed, not used to being challenged like this. Especially not by Della. "What are you talking about?" she said, tossing her hair back over her shoulders.

"You're always making fun of her, and it's horrible," Della said, realizing that she didn't feel the least bit intimidated by Melanie anymore. It was an empowering sensation. "You don't know anything about Iceland or what it's like over there." Della folded her arms, not letting her gaze slide away. "Why does it matter where Katrin comes from anyway? She has as much right to be here as any of us. Just leave her alone."

Katrin raised her head and gave Della an astonished smile.

"You can't talk to me that way," Melanie said.

"Yes I can, Melanie. I am Della Dupree." It sounded so good that Della laughed and said it again. "I'm Della Dupree."

"You're weird," Melanie muttered.

"And we're not being mean," Cassie said, twisting some hair around her finger. "It's just fun."

"Would you like it if I made fun of your clothes and where you live and what you like to eat?" Della said. "Because I call that bullying."

"Della's right," Anna broke in. "You are horrible to poor Katrin."

"I think you're all being oversensitive," Melanie said, turning to walk away. "Come on, Cassie." And the girls slunk off toward history class.

"Thank you!" Katrin said, beaming at Della.

"You should sit with us at lunch," Sophie suggested. "I'm sorry we didn't ask you before, Katrin."

"That's okay." Katrin shrugged. "And I'd like that."

"What happened in the library?" Anna whispered in Della's ear. "You seem so different."

"The library! I have to get my bag," Della said, racing down the corridor. "I'll see you in history," she called back over her shoulder.

• • •

"I thought there was a fire, the way you dashed out of here," Miss Dickenson said. And then, rather frostily: "You can't leave valuable books like that lying around, Della."

"I know, and I'm so sorry, Miss Dickenson. It won't happen again."

The librarian sniffed the air and gave Della a strange look. "What have you been doing? You've been gone less than five minutes?"

"I am sorry, Miss Dickenson, but I really need to go," Della said, rushing over to the table she'd been working at. "I have a presentation I can't be late for."

As Della crouched down to grab her backpack, she noticed that the table legs were beautifully carved, with vines and leaves twisting up them. Running her fingers over the delicate carvings, she saw a tiny acorn etched into the top of one of the legs. "Ivan!" Della whispered, knowing right away he had made this.

"Do you know how old that table is, Miss Dickenson?" Della asked, hurrying toward the door. "The big one I was sitting at."

"Thirteenth century, as far as I know," the librarian replied. "It's lovely, isn't it?"

"Yes it is," Della agreed, delighted that Ivan had been able to follow his passion.

She was late getting to class, and Miss Barlow did not look too happy as Della slipped into the room. "We are about to start our presentations, Miss Dupree. Perhaps you would like to go first?"

Della nodded, and instead of going to her desk, she walked to the front of the room. Not quite sure what she was going to do (because she certainly couldn't perform a transformation spell and turn the class into hares) and ignoring the fact that she smelled like a ripe barnyard, Della stood for a moment, staring into space.

"Ready, Della?" Miss Barlow prompted.

Della cleared her throat. "My name is Della Dupree," she began, "and I'm a witch. Every day I wake up and I wish that I wasn't. Not because I have to eat horrible pottage and can't take baths and have to sleep on the floor, but because I'm terrified of being found out. You hate me because I'm different, and it's the worst feeling in the world, being hated just for being myself." She caught Melanie's eye and refused to look away until Melanie looked down at her desk. "I'm not evil or dangerous. I'm just like everyone else, even if I have to take away your thoughts and turn you into a rat to survive." Della held her chin up, a great sense of pride racing through her. "I want to help people, but you won't let me. You put me in a dungeon because you don't understand." Della gave a shiver, remembering how awful it had felt, being locked away in the dark. "If you bothered to get to know me, then you'd see how wonderful witches are, the amazing things magic can do." Della paused a moment before spreading out her arms and chanting, "Twelve twenty-three, twelve twenty-three, Ruthersfield was founded by Witch Dupree." And then, because she couldn't help herself, she finished up: "And Witch Dupree is me!"

"Well." Miss Barlow picked a speck of lint off her cloak. "That was certainly getting into the spirit of things."

"Except she wouldn't have practiced mind magic or transformation spells," Cassie pointed out. "Those things are so dangerous."

"Well, it may be stretching our imaginations a bit, but you never know," Miss Barlow suggested. "It was a very different time."

"And Witch Dupree wasn't thrown in a dungeon," Melanie said. "It doesn't say that anywhere."

"Maybe that's just how she felt," Katrin offered. "Trapped in a dungeon because no one understood her."

"Good point, Katrin," Miss Barlow said, "and a very creative presentation, Della."

Before lunch Della announced that she was going to go and talk to Ms. Cray about setting up an animal-magic program. After all, Ivan had been brave enough to follow his passion, so the least she could do was try to follow hers.

"Can't believe you're actually going to face the evil headmistress," Sophie said.

Della grinned. "That's what Witch Dupree would have done."

Ms. Cray was sitting behind her desk, and she looked surprised to see Della come in.

"And to what do I owe this honor, Miss Dupree?"

Della didn't reply. She was staring at a picture hanging above the headmistress's desk.

"I moved it there because you couldn't see it in the corner, but now I'm having second thoughts," Ms. Cray confessed. "It's a little too much in the light, don't you think? I know why our founder has been hidden in a dark corner for so long."

"It's . . ." Della couldn't believe this was Ivan's sketch of her. Hanging in the headmistress's office. But it was. There was no mistaking that misshapen head, pointy nose, and lopsided eyes. And the smudgy charcoal lines made her look about thirty. Someone had fastened a plaque to the bottom of the frame that said DELLA DUPREE—FOUNDER OF RUTHERSFIELD ACADEMY—1223.

"Interesting." Ms. Cray tilted her head a little to the left, examining Della and then looking back at the portrait. "There is a slight resemblance between you and your namesake. Something about the eyes, I think."

"I really don't see it at all," Della said, but she couldn't help feeling rather proud.

Much to Della's surprise, Ms. Cray didn't dismiss the idea of introducing an animal-magic program into Ruthersfield. She didn't agree to it either, but that was better than Della had hoped for, and when she was in year ten, Della finally got her wish. The old potions lab was turned into an animal center where the first dragon egg was hatched. It had been found, abandoned, beside the old railway tracks at Little Shamlington, and Della had insisted they try to hatch it, wrapping the egg in layers of thistledown and keeping it warm in a cauldron of sunshine.

Della went on to become head girl, and after leaving Ruthersfield, she set up a groundbreaking organization to bring back extinct animals, managing to reintroduce the dodo in 2035. Although they weren't the smartest creatures, Della discovered that they made excellent pets and became known for their extremely loving and loyal personalities. True to her history, she also became the first witch ambassador at the United Nations, using her magic to weave peace between countries and mending many a feud with a pot of her famous lasagna.

Della and Katrin became firm friends, and (much to Della's delight) Katrin knitted special wing warmers for all Della's baby bats. To no one's great surprise, when Katrin grew up, she became the first Icelandic witch to win a Noblet prize, inventing a special knitted cover that could be spread across the earth's atmosphere, regulating the temperature of the planet so it wouldn't overheat.

There were many times Della thought about going back to see how Dame Bessie and the others were doing. But she didn't want to risk getting stuck there again, and (more importantly) Della was anxious about what she'd find. Because sometimes knowing was even worse than not knowing, as after a trip to the local library one day Della discovered that Castle Hepworth did indeed burn down. But not until the fifteenth century, when one of the cooks managed to set fire to a pie in the castle kitchens.

Della did know, from reading her history of magic book, that Elizabeth Ruthersfield taught at the school until she was 102, and that the first class to graduate included Willow Reynolds of Deckle Mead, Mary

Dutton of Potts Bottom, Gwyneth Brooker of Little Shamlington, and Faye Cox of Pig Hollow. As to what happened to Della Dupree? Well, the textbook couldn't tell her much. It was rumored that Witch Dupree had sailed to the Spanish colonies, where some believed she might have come from. And there was talk that she went to live in the Highlands of Scotland and train dragons, and even a suggestion (which made Della blush when she read it) that she had married a local lord's son! Of course only one person knew what really happened, and that was Della Dupree herself!

Della's Tips for Time Travel

In case you find yourself with a time-travel pendant and would like to take a trip back into the past, here are some tips that Della wished she had known about before visiting the Middle Ages. Ask an adult for permission and/or to help you to set up and use kitchen equipment, crack eggs, cut with knives, or take pans in and out of the oven, etc.

Lemon Poppy Seed Muffins

Makes 12-14 muffins

It is important not to time-travel on an empty stomach, since you never quite know what to expect and where your next meal will be coming from. So try to have breakfast before you leave and perhaps take an extra muffin along with you in case hunger strikes. These lemon poppy seed muffins are some of Della's favorites. She often stops in at Poppy's bakery on her way to school and can never resist the lemon-glazed muffins that Poppy always makes to celebrate the start of spring.

~ INGREDIENTS ~

1¾ cups all-purpose flour

1½ teaspoons baking powder

½ teaspoon baking soda

¼ + ⅛ teaspoons salt

⅔ cup sugar

2 tablespoons poppy seeds

2 eggs

¾ cup plain whole milk yogurt

6 tablespoons butter, melted

zest of 2 lemons, grated

¼ cup lemon juice

Lemon syrup for the tops:

¼ cup lemon juice

¼ cup sugar

1 tablespoon water

~ Method ~

. . . .

1. Preheat oven to 375°F. Put muffin liners in tin.
2. In a small bowl, blend together the flour, baking powder, baking soda, salt, sugar, and poppy seeds.
3. In another, larger bowl, mix the eggs, yogurt, melted butter, lemon zest, and juice. Beat thoroughly. Add the dry ingredients and mix until just blended. The mixture will be thick, but don't overbeat because this will make your muffins tough.
4. Spoon the batter into the prepared muffin cups. Bake about 15–20 minutes, until a toothpick inserted into the center of a muffin comes out clean.
5. While the muffins bake, prepare the syrup. Combine the lemon juice, sugar, and water in a small saucepan. Bring

to a boil and boil for 1 minute. Set aside.

6. When the muffins are done, gently poke holes in the tops with a fork and drizzle syrup evenly over each muffin. Let cool in the pan a few minutes and serve warm. Of course they are excellent cold, too, in case you happen to be time-traveling.

7. Enjoy!

A Really Tasty Pottage

Della found the medieval pottage disgusting, and since it turns up at most medieval meals, it is an excellent idea to know how to make a pot of this extremely tasty soup, just in case you find yourself back there. Most of the ingredients can be found in a medieval kitchen, but feel free to substitute if things like potatoes have not yet been discovered. Not only will this soup wow your medieval hosts, but it will also mean you don't have to go to bed hungry!

~ INGREDIENTS ~

2 tablespoons olive oil

1 large onion, diced

3 cloves garlic, minced

1–2 stalks celery, chopped (If you don't like celery in your soup, leave it out. Della hates it!)

2 carrots, sliced

3 cups mixed chopped vegetables, your choice (Try cauliflower, zucchini, broccoli, green beans, corn kernels,

potatoes, turnips—whatever is around.)

½ teaspoon salt

1 bay leaf

sprinkle of chopped fresh herbs, optional (Use whatever you like. Della usually puts in parsley and basil.)

8 cups vegetable broth

1 15-ounce can chopped tomatoes (Again, this is optional as some people simply don't like tomatoes in their vegetable soup.)

1 15-ounce can of cannellini beans or a cup of dried lentils, also optional—but a good source of protein

~ METHOD ~

. . . .

1. Heat oil in a large pot over medium heat. Add the diced onion, garlic, celery (if using), and carrots. Cook gently without burning for about 5 minutes, until onions are soft.

2. Add the rest of the vegetables, stir, and sprinkle with salt. Cook for another few minutes—to soften, not to color.

3. Add bay leaf and herbs, stirring to coat the vegetables well.

4. Add vegetable broth. Then add tomatoes and beans or lentils, if using, and bring to a simmer. Cook for 45

minutes to an hour. If you like your vegetables crunchy, you can cook for less time. Taste, and add more seasoning if needed.

5. Remove the bay leaf and serve your homemade vegetable soup with a sprinkle of Parmesan cheese and a nice hunk of crusty bread to dip in!

World Peace Lasagna

Even though it is a little cumbersome to bring along a dish of lasagna when you time-travel, Della strongly recommends it (unless you have access to a wand and can magic up a pot using the italiomama spell), because this hearty dish can get you out of many a difficult situation. Served up to warring armies, it can bring about peace and will put a smile on the crankiest person's face. This was a huge hit with Lord Hepworth and his brother, James, and if you happen to lose your time-travel pendant and can't get back to where you came from, then feel free to eat the whole pan of lasagna yourself!

~ INGREDIENTS ~

2 tablespoons olive oil

1 large onion, finely chopped

4 garlic cloves, finely minced

1 pound ground beef

1 15-ounce can chopped tomatoes

salt and pepper, to taste

1 bay leaf

4 tablespoons butter

⅓ cup all-purpose flour

2½ cups whole milk

1 cup grated Parmesan cheese, or more to taste, plus 3
tablespoons for the top

About 9 sheets dried no-boil lasagna pasta, depending on the
size of the sheets and your dish (You'll need 3 layers of
pasta.)

~ METHOD ~

. . . .

1. Heat the oil in a large, heavy-bottom frying pan over a
medium heat, and gently fry the onion and garlic until
softened. Turn the heat up a little, add the ground beef,
and cook until browned all over.

2. Pour in the chopped tomatoes; fill the empty can ¼ full
of water and add that; season with salt, pepper, and bay
leaf; then bring to a simmer. Cover partially, turn the heat
down, and leave to simmer gently for about an hour.

3. Preheat the oven to 400°F.

4. To make the béchamel sauce, melt the butter on medium
to low heat in a medium pan and then whisk in the flour.
Cook for a couple of minutes, stirring; then gradually

whisk in the milk and bring to a boil. Turn the heat down to low and continue to stir. Simmer for 5 minutes until thickened. Stir in the grated Parmesan and season with salt and pepper.

5. To assemble the lasagna, take a deep, wide casserole dish and coat the bottom with a third of the meat sauce, topped with a quarter of the béchamel, and finally a layer of pasta. Repeat two more layers, and then top the last layer of pasta with the rest of the béchamel and the remaining parmesan.

6. Cook in oven for about 45 minutes to an hour, until golden and bubbling.

A Sweet-Smelling Pomander Ball

Since people didn't wash very often in medieval times, and the smells could get rather overwhelming, it might be a good idea to bring a pomander ball along with you when you time-travel. The sweet scent of cloves and orange zest will help mask any powerful odors, which, if you are heading into the thirteenth century, you are bound to encounter on your trip.

~ MATERIALS ~

1 firm orange

whole cloves

ribbon, if you'd like to hang your pomander

~ METHOD ~

1. Stud whole cloves all over an orange, making a pattern, or until the orange is completely covered. If you are having trouble sticking the cloves in, use a toothpick to

make the holes first. Be creative and arrange the cloves in diamond, circular, or other patterns. As the orange dries, it will release a delicate, spicy fragrance.

2. Next tie a pretty ribbon around it, making sure you include a loop to hang it from. Dangle in a place that could do with some freshening up!

    Note: If you want your pomander to last, store it in a paper bag for a few weeks. Use lots of cloves, which are a natural preserving agent. The cloves will draw out the juices, and the orange will shrink in size.

Homemade Jester's Hat

To enter into the spirit of castle life, you can whip up one of these jester's hats to wear. People in the Middle Ages loved being entertained, so if you are looking to make friends, put on your hat and turn a few somersaults, and you will find yourself the life and soul of the party. Knowing a few card tricks can't hurt either, so you might want to practice some on your family and friends before you start time-traveling. Pulling a coin out of someone's ear always gets a laugh!

~ Materials ~

Any paper will do (Feel free to recycle old drawings, as this will make your jester hat nice and colorful.)
Scissors, tape, and glue

~ Method ~

1. Begin by making a headband out of paper, but don't tape the ends together yet. The headband should be about 4

inches wide and long enough to fit around your head with a 1-inch overlap.

2. Now cut 6 paper triangles, each with a 2-inch-wide base and around 10 inches high. You can color them different colors or draw patterns on them if you like. It's up to you.

3. Tape the base end of each triangle, evenly spaced, along the top inside edge of the headband. Fold the triangles so they flop over the outside of the headband to make it look like a jester's hat. Tape the two edges of the headband together so that it fits on your head.

4. Cut out small circles about an inch wide and glue one onto the top point of each triangle. These are your bells! They won't jingle, but they look fun!

Homemade Magic Wands

Magic was much more common in medieval times, so if you are traveling back there, you may find it stirs up magic you didn't know you possessed and you are actually able to cast spells. Depending on when you were born, you will have a stronger connection to particular types of wood. Find your birth month below and use the wood that fits you best (documented by the first high priestess of magic in her guide to witchcraft). Remember: Be very careful when you cast your spells, as natural wands can be extremely powerful. So PROCEED WITH CAUTION.

January — Oak

February — Ash

March — Cherry

April — Pear

May — Apple

June — Beech

July — Alder

August — Chestnut

September—Maple
October—Birch
November—Hawthorn
December—Holly

Stripping the bark from your wand will make for a smoother flow of magic. Feel free to wind ribbons around the handle and decorate with jewels, feathers, or whatever you would like.

~ Acknowledgments ~
. . . .

Thanks to Ann Tobias, my brilliant agent, for all her support and guidance. To Paula Wiseman, my equally brilliant editor, and the entire Simon & Schuster team.

Thanks to Chloë Foglia for her beautiful book design, and Seb Mesnard for his gorgeous illustration of Della.

A huge thank-you to my sister Annabelle for reading many early drafts, helping me work out the kinks, and patiently explaining how time travel works!

Thanks to Jane Gilbert Keith for her excellent feedback.

I am so grateful to Dale Fisher for sending me an email suggesting I write Witch Dupree's story—so thank you, thank you, Dale!!

As always, many thanks to my parents for reading each chapter as I wrote it, and putting up with my daily phone calls!

And last but never least, thanks to Jon, Sebastian, Oliver, Ben, and Juliette—I'd time-travel with all of you, anywhere!!